WINTER
COMES

Word Association Publishers
205 Fifth Avenue
Tarentum, Pennsylvania 15084
www.wordassociation.com
1.800.827.7903

ISBN: 978-1-63385-271-6
Library of Congress Control Number: 2018910101

Design and Layout by
Jason Price

Printed in the United States of America.

WINTER
COMES

A TUESDAY TABLE LADIES' MYSTERY

OCTAVIA LONG

To Dorothy Armistead—
Our Friend and Colleague
A Tuesday Table Lady who continues to inspire us

Acknowledgments

This book is the result of the urgings we have received from readers of *Where's Laura?* our first book. We are grateful for the kind reception and enthusiasm of both our Longwood at Oakmont community and many organizations in Western Pennsylvania at whose invitation we have spoken about our writing adventures. It has been so pleasing to learn how much a story about the joyful side of vintage years has meant to our readers.

We are grateful for the support and guidance of our publishers, Tom and Francine Costello of Word Association Publishers, and their designer, Jason Price. We are especially indebted to our editor, Marty McHugh, for his cheerful patience and helpful suggestions.

We are pleased that the Presbyterian Senior Care Foundation Longwood Benevolent Care Fund is the recipient in perpetuity of the net proceeds of the books for the assistance of residents with financial needs.

We are indebted to a generous full-page article by Marylynne Pitz in the *Pittsburgh Post-Gazette* about the creation of *Where's Laura?* We have been astounded by its broad impact.

If Winter comes, can Spring be far behind?

—PERCY BYSSHE SHELLY

Contents

	Characters xii
1	Prologue xiii
1	A Blizzard 1
2	News Travels 21
3	Trouble at Oakwood 41
4	About Time 55
5	Creative Dining 67
6	Another Robbery? 81
7	The Absent Chef 91
8	Welcome Home 105
9	Mysteries 123
10	Robert's Discovery 139
11	Disturbing News 145
12	A Night Out 161
13	New Information 171
14	Aspiring Writers 181
15	Answers 191
16	Surprise 203
	Epilogue 213
	About the Authors 215

Characters

TUESDAY TABLE LADIES

Sandra Brown—*consultant in information science*

Barbara Jackson—*lawyer and homemaker*

Laura Lambert—*lawyer*

Ellen Moore—*high-school math teacher*

Harriet Parker—*social worker*

Karen Taylor—*columnist*

OTHER RESIDENTS

Robert Symonds—*former State Department officer*

Elizabeth Cutler

OAKWOOD STAFF

Catherine Evans—*executive director*

Augusta—*housekeeper*

Nora— *housekeeper*

Emily—*dining room server*

Kevin—*dining room server*

Frank—*chef*

OTHER

Steve O'Malley—*FBI agent*

Prologue

The snow swirled around a dark figure that slowly emerged from the mist. Stopping before one of the cottages that was lit by a porchlight, the man studied the number on the door. "Yes," he murmured to himself. He slowly moved along the side of the cottage to a lit window. He pressed his face against the glass and peered into the room watching as a man entered.

The man quickly moved across the room to a small chest where he removed a revolver from a drawer. Opening a closet door, he placed the gun in a case on the shelf, carefully locked it, and closed the door.

The loud honk of a horn broke the early morning silence, and the lights in the room went off. The figure quickly moved from the window and crouched behind a large shrub. He saw the porch light turned off and the man coming out of the house. The man stepped off the small porch and headed for the waiting taxi. The driver helped him put his large duffle in the trunk. The two men got into the vehicle. It slowly pulled away from the curb.

The figure watched the taxi disappear in the falling snow. He hesitated slightly before moving to the front of the darkened cottage. As he carefully examined the building and its surroundings, he heard a snowplow moving down the street toward him, and he quickly moved away from the cottage. *Not now*, he thought. *I'll come back later.*

He strode to a parking lot a short distance away, climbed into a dark sedan, and slowly drove off.

CHAPTER ONE

A Blizzard

Snowflakes are one of nature's most fragile things, but just look at what they can do when they stick together.

—VESTA M. KELLY

"It's still coming down," Harriet said gloomily as she looked out at the darkening sky.

"Yes, it's been snowing all day. I thought it was supposed to stop by now," replied Laura. "I have to admit, it's such a beautiful scene that I've been watching it out of the window when there were other things I should have been doing."

The two women sat at their usual table near the window in the Riverview dining room. They were soon joined by Barbara and Ellen, two other residents of the Oakwood Retirement Village. "Look how hard it's snowing now," said Barbara as she sat. "I guess it shouldn't be surprising since we're well into January."

"You're right," said Ellen. "We've had almost no snow up till now. Does anyone know if Robert managed to get away this morning?"

"I saw him get into a taxi first thing this morning," replied Harriet, whose cottage was next door to Robert's. "The roads seemed to be fairly clear then, but I'm afraid they're probably in bad shape by now. He got away to Florida just in time to miss the storm. But I was sorry to see him go – my cottage seems a little isolated now that he's gone."

The last two members of the Tuesday Table, Karen and Sandra, appeared and took their seats.

Emily, their usual server, quickly approached the table to pass out menus and take their drink orders. Sandra's bottle of Pinot Grigio was taken to the kitchen to be opened while the women studied their dinner menus.

"Oh dear," murmured Barbara. "I'm torn between the braised lamb shank and the crab-stuffed sole."

"Me too," said Ellen. "I like them both."

"I always thought the meals were good, but they seem to be even better in the last few months since the new chef started," Sandra remarked.

Emily returned with the opened wine and jotted down their orders as it drew darker outside the large window next to their table.

"Okay you all. Now that we're all here, we need to decide. Are we going to take up Robert's suggestion?" asked Barbara.

"I don't know. The idea that the six of us could write a mystery novel seems pretty ridiculous to me," Harriet grumbled. "Just because he's writing a book about his Foreign Service experiences in Russia, he seems to think we should write a book too. None of us have ever done anything like that before."

"I've written my Helpful Hints column for years," Karen said somewhat defensively, "and Barbara has written book reviews for the Oakwood magazine."

"And we've all read a ton of mysteries," Ellen said.

"But most important, we actually solved a mystery ourselves – that's why Robert suggested we could write one," said Barbara.

"I think it was sheer luck that we managed to figure out where Laura was, and besides, we had help from Robert," Harriet replied.

"But Harriet, we did a lot of research on the internet and here at Oakwood before we tracked her down to that Pennsylvania farmhouse," Sandra said.

"Yes, my father and I were impressed with your persistence and your internet research skills," Laura added.

"I see Robert's suggestion as a challenge," Sandra said. "If he can do it, why can't we? I think we should at least give it a try."

"We'd need a good plot, and characters, and a setting," Karen said thoughtfully.

"We'll have to think about this. It would be a lot of work," Ellen said. "I'm going to the salad bar. Anyone else going?"

"I am," said Laura as she rose.

The others remained at the table while Sandra passed around the wine and Emily served their soups and salads. Their conversation drifted to other topics.

"Just before I came to dinner, I heard another weather alert. Apparently, they're predicting significantly more snow tonight," said Sandra. "The storm was expected to move on north by now, but it has stalled in the Mid-Atlantic region and could produce a lot more snow tonight and tomorrow."

"Oh dear," exclaimed Barbara. "I was planning to go shopping tomorrow. I need some painting supplies for my watercolor demonstration at the Friday art class."

"And I have a history seminar at the community college tomorrow afternoon," said Karen. "I'd really hate to miss it."

"They'll probably cancel classes if it's as bad as they're predicting," Sandra said. "Don't forget we have a meeting with Frank about the dining menu first thing in the morning," she told Karen, who nodded.

Ellen and Laura joined in the conversation when they returned to the table. It seemed everyone had plans the storm might jeopardize. They continued to discuss the sudden change in weather through dinner.

"I was thinking how pretty the snow looked," said Laura. "Everything's so quiet and peaceful under a coat of snow, but now I guess it may become a real problem."

"It's a problem I'm happy to have. Remember how excited we were as children when we had snow days?" Sandra asked. "I feel like that now. I can think of all sorts of things I'd like to do tomorrow if we get snowed in."

"You're right," Barbara responded. "It's like having an unexpected day off."

"Almost a holiday," Ellen said smiling. "Of course, it can be hard to get here to the dining room if there's a lot of snow. Fortunately, the path was pretty clear tonight. I hope it's still okay when we leave. I do like eating here so much more than in the dining room in Oak Hall."

The Oakwood Retirement Village included several buildings besides the original plantation house called Oak Hall. In addition to the apartments and cottages where the residents lived, there were a health care center, a recreation center, and the Riverview dining room. The cottages and the Riverview, unlike most of the other buildings, were not attached to Oak Hall; they were a short distance away overlooking the river that emptied into the Chesapeake Bay a few miles downstream.

The large majority of Oakwood residents, like those in other retirement communities, lived very independent lives coming and going to a variety of activities within and outside the community. They enjoyed the fact they had no snow to shovel or grass to cut, and delicious meals were prepared for them in the two dining rooms. They were free of many of the chores that made life difficult for those in their later years but were still able to live quite independently. If illness or disability did strike, they could move into the health care units that could provide the services they required.

Each of the Tuesday Table Ladies, as they were called by the other residents, had moved to Oakwood sometime after a divorce or a death of a husband. Some of them had children living nearby, but others had children scattered across the country. Their friends at Oakwood were like a second family, and they had grown quite close since joining the Tuesday Table. They all looked forward to their weekly dinners together, and there was usually lots of laughter coming from their table.

The conversation turned to the food in front of them as Emily served their entrees. "This lamb shank is amazing – I don't think I've ever tasted a better one," said Karen. "I can't figure out some of the ingredients he's used. There's an unusual spice I can't identify. Did anyone else get the lamb?"

"I did, and you're right. It's really delicious and a little different from the usual braised lamb," Barbara replied. "Chef Frank is so good that I'm surprised he isn't working in a fancy restaurant in Washington or New York."

"Well anyway, he's a great chef, and we're lucky to have him. I just hope he stays here and doesn't go off to a more lucrative position," Harriet said.

"Yes, a lot of the residents' families eat here from time to time," said Karen. "I'm afraid they might recommend him to an upscale restaurant or club elsewhere."

Emily returned to clear the table and offer dessert. "Tonight, we have a white chocolate raspberry cake or a cappuccino crunch ice cream sundae."

With three orders for cake, two ice creams, and one "Just decaf, please," Emily headed back to the kitchen.

She returned almost immediately. She appeared quite flustered. "Kevin will finish serving you tonight. We've been told that River Road will be closed shortly, and we need to get out of here while we can. Kevin lives close enough to walk home, so he's volunteered to stay to clear the tables and help out in the kitchen."

"Be careful going home, Emily. How are you getting there?" Laura asked.

"The Oakwood shuttle bus will take us home because public transportation has already closed down."

"Be careful, dear," Harriet said as Emily hurried away.

Kevin appeared shortly with dessert, coffee, and tea. After serving the six of them, he moved on to clear other tables. Apparently, he was the only server left in the dining room. Fortunately for him, Riverview had not been as crowded as usual for a Tuesday night since a number of residents had decided to stay in the Oak Hall dining room rather than braving the storm to reach Riverview.

"Do you think we'll have a problem getting back to Oak Hall?" asked Ellen. "It's been snowing pretty heavily all through dinner."

"I'm sure they've kept the path clear enough for us to get back," Barbara replied soothingly.

"They could always pick us up in the golf carts the maintenance department uses and ferry us back to the main building," joked Sandra. "That might be fun."

"Fun for you maybe. I'm not sure I could climb into one of those carts," Karen said unhappily.

They stopped in the coatroom for coats, hats, and scarves. They had all worn winter boots for the walk between the buildings, so they felt well prepared to step back into the snow-covered landscape. What they were not ready for was the strong wind that whipped between the buildings and tugged at their hats and scarves. They grabbed onto each other for support and made their way to the main building as quickly as they could.

"Wow! I didn't think it would be that bad," muttered Karen as she shook off the snow that clung to the bottom of her cane. "I thought I was going to be knocked over by that wind."

"Yes, I don't envy the staff members who have to go home tonight. I'd think some of them might want to stay here until tomorrow," said Laura.

"I'm not sure it'll be any better tomorrow," Sandra said. "The weather report I heard indicated that this might keep up until Thursday morning. If that's the case, we could get quite an accumulation of snow – very unusual for this part of the country."

"Thanks to global warming," Barbara grumbled.

"I'd hardly call this 'warming'," replied Harriet sarcastically.

"That's why they call it 'climate change'," Karen retorted.

Sandra moved over to a couch in front of the lobby fireplace. "Let's sit by the fire and warm up for a while before we head to our apartments. How are you going to get to your cottage, Harriet?"

Harriet was the only one of the Tuesday Table Ladies who lived in one of the cottages scattered along the riverfront.

"The shuttle will drop me off at my door when I'm ready to go back out again. That's why I came to Oak Hall with you all. I didn't want to walk across the lawn from Riverview to my cottage."

The six women settled into chairs and on the couches around the fireplace and talked about their disrupted plans for the following day.

"Thank goodness I'm on library duty so I don't have to go off the campus tomorrow anyway," Harriet said. "I assume the shuttle will be running, so I can get back and forth, but I certainly hope this clears up by Friday. I have a speaker driving out from Washington, and I'll have to cancel the lecture if he can't make it."

"I bet my history class will be cancelled," said Karen. "If so, I can use the time to take care of some chores around my apartment. It could be fun to get snowed in."

"I'm sure we can all make good use of a free day," agreed Sandra. "There never seems to be enough time for all the things we want to do."

"I might just take the day off and read a novel," said Laura happily. "That would be a real treat. A snow day would be like a surprise present from Mother Nature. A free day to do whatever we want. No classes or lectures or other responsibilities."

"I could spend the whole day painting. There just never seems to be enough time to try some of the new techniques I've been reading about," Barbara said eagerly.

"And it's always so satisfying to sit in front of a nice fire while it's storming outside," added Ellen snuggling into her chair.

The fireplace was in the center of a large, well-lit lobby that was comfortably furnished with easy chairs, couches, and tables with lamps and a variety of newspapers and magazines. Residents were slowly exiting the dining room just off the lobby; some stopped at the desk to chat with Joe, the clerk on night duty. Those who lived in cottages sat near the entrance to await the return of the Oakwood shuttle bus, which had taken home the staff members who usually came by public transportation or who were afraid to drive on the snow-covered roads on such a treacherous night.

A sudden commotion at the lobby entrance – Alex, the shuttle driver, came in with a blast of cold air as the sliding door remained open for an instant.

"Whew! Am I ever glad to get back here. It's very bad out there," he said addressing Joe and the residents waiting to be driven to their cottages. Seeing their looks of alarm, he hastened to add, "Oh, we can get to the cottages all right. I'll take you home in a few minutes. It's River Road and the back roads that are almost impassable. In fact, they're closing off River Road now – I passed a big pileup about a mile down the road. A pickup truck had skidded into a car, which was pushed into another car and so forth. I don't even know how many vehicles were involved – there were so many police cars there that it was hard to see what was going on. I'm just glad to have gotten back here in one piece."

"I guess I'd better head home while Alex is still driving," said Harriet as she rose. "Our maintenance people do a good job of keeping our driveway pretty clear, but this may become too much even for them to deal with. I'll probably see you all tomorrow unless I get snowed in." She joined the other residents at the door, and Alex led them out to the waiting shuttle.

The other five women remained seated. The fire was very inviting after their brief sojourn outside. It was still early; they weren't quite ready to go to their apartments.

"There's something I wanted to talk to you all about, but I've been afraid you might laugh at me. I'm sure Harriet would disapprove, so this might be a good time to bring it up while she isn't here." Sandra took a deep breath before continuing. "I'm thinking of joining an online dating service for older adults."

She was met with open mouths and looks of disbelief.

"Are you serious?" asked an astonished Ellen.

"I can't believe it," Karen said slowly.

"Which one did you want to join?" asked Laura curiously.

"It's called About Time, and it caters to people sixty and over," Sandra replied somewhat defensively.

"Why on earth do you feel you need to join a dating service?" Barbara asked. "There are single men here at Oakwood."

"I know, but it seems to me that as soon as you have dinner with someone here, all sorts of rumors start, and the next thing you know, you're treated as a couple even if you don't hit it off with him and you decide never to have dinner with him again. Or even worse, you like him as a friend and enjoy spending time with him, but everyone thinks it's a romantic relationship even if it's purely platonic. I wanted to explore other possibilities and have a little privacy as well."

"Well?" Ellen prompted her.

"I have a cousin who met her husband on a dating site, and she assured me that they were pretty safe as long as you're careful and use your head. I'm not interested in another husband – heaven forbid – but it would be nice to find a companion to go to movies, plays, concerts, and such. It's just nice to have male company now and then, not that you ladies aren't great company," Sandra said with an uncertain laugh.

"How does it work?" asked Laura. "Dating services always seemed sort of risky to me."

"Actually, they operate in different ways. Some you don't join at first. You sign on only to create a personal profile for yourself – what your interests are, what you like and don't like, some of your personal habits like drinking or smoking, and so on. The service posts pictures of men who have similar interests and may be compatible along with their data. I can choose to post a 'like' on any of them, but there's no way the men can contact me or I can contact them. You must join the service and pay your fee. Then they'll help make the contact with your choices if any. I haven't found any I like so far."

"That sounds pretty safe to me up to this point, but how would you manage getting together to meet?" Laura asked.

"I guess you'd arrange to meet in a public place for coffee or lunch or something. I haven't gotten that far yet. Don't worry. I'd be very careful," Sandra assured them smiling.

"The whole idea still sounds risky to me," Karen said.

"I suppose they'd all be honest about their ages and habits, but what if they sent a picture that was twenty years old? How are you to know?" asked Laura.

"It sounds like fun to me as long as you're anonymous I guess," said Ellen. "I'd love to see what kind of men show up on the site."

"Come on up to my apartment and I'll show you the profiles I've received. I'd love to know what you think about them. Do you all want to come too?"

"I'm going to go back to my apartment. I have a few things I'd like to do before bedtime," Karen said. She had no interest in Sandra's project – it all sounded so strange to her.

"No thanks. I'm too comfortable here in front of the fireplace to get up," replied Barbara. She felt the chance of online dating at her age was a real long shot and not worth spending time on. Besides, she knew she would never meet another man who measured up to her late husband.

"Me too," said Laura lazily. "It's so nice to sit next to the fire when it's so nasty outside."

The three apartment buildings – Albemarle, Baltimore, and Calvert – were attached to Oak Hall by enclosed and covered walkways so the residents could move easily from one to another in bad weather. Oak Hall, a large, redbrick building with tall, white columns and shutters had been converted from a plantation house to a retirement community some twenty years earlier, and the apartment buildings had been added at that time. The two-bedroom cottages along the river and the Riverview dining room were added a short time later. The health care center and recreation center had been built more recently, and like the apartments, they were attached to Oak Hall by enclosed walkways.

Sandra and Ellen headed to Sandra's apartment while Karen made her way to her apartment and Laura and Barbara kept their comfortable seats near the fireplace. They had known each other longer than any of the other Tuesday Table Ladies. Both were lawyers, and they had started out in the same firm many years before, occasionally working on cases together.

Over the years, Barbara turned her attention to her growing family and became active in the PTA and other school activities while Laura and her husband, who had no children, focused instead on work and an active social life.

Eventually, Laura had moved to another community, and they had lost track of each other. Thus it was a happy surprise for Laura to find Barbara at Oakwood when she moved in. The two had quickly reconnected and were good friends.

"What do you think of Sandra's latest project?" asked Barbara.

"Oh, it's probably harmless," Laura replied. "Sandra enjoys having admirers around her, and she's so attractive and young looking that she can still find men to fill the role. She's smart. I don't think she'll do anything foolish. It's kind of nice to see her excited about something. Did you see her eyes light up when she talked about it?"

"I guess you're right. Besides, we can keep an eye on her and make sure she doesn't do something silly."

"Beautiful as it is, I'm a little concerned about this storm. A lot of people could be hurt if it's as bad as it sounds. If the power goes out, we have generators here, but there are a lot of families in the area that could be in trouble," Laura said.

They sat quietly, lost in their thoughts while watching the fire. The lobby was almost deserted. Residents had gone to their apartments or been driven to their cottages by Alex, who had returned. He and Joe were chatting at the desk. Both would be on duty as security all night ready to respond if a problem arose.

Laura got up and went to the window to study the conditions outside. "It looks bad out there. The driveway is completely buried now. I don't see anything moving on River Road. I think I'm ready to go home."

Laura and Barbara headed for their apartments hoping for a snow day the next day when they were stopped by one of the security guards who regularly patrolled the buildings. "Good evening, Mark," said Laura. "I hope you're managing to keep dry and warm in all this snow."

"Oh yes, Mrs. Lambert," he replied with a smile. "I'm glad I ran into you though. I want to warn you about what happened earlier today. They haven't officially notified anyone yet, so almost no one's heard about it, but it'll probably be all over the campus tomorrow."

"What is it, Mark?" asked Barbara. "It sounds serious."

"I'm afraid it may be. One of the residents in your building was robbed today. It seems someone broke into her apartment and some expensive jewelry was taken."

"Oh no!" said Laura.

"Be sure your door is locked when you go out. She swears that she locked her door, but if someone got into a locked apartment, that would be even worse."

The women stared at him in astonishment. There had never been a robbery at Oakwood since they had been there.

"Oh dear," whispered Barbara. "Poor thing. What floor does she live on?"

"She's on the second floor down at the end of the hall and next to the stairway. It's pretty quiet and secluded there. No one has reported seeing a stranger in the building. I don't suppose you two noticed anything out of the ordinary today?"

"No, nothing," said Laura, "but I think I would like to get back to my apartment to make sure everything's okay."

"Me too," said Barbara.

"Sure," replied Mark. "Just let me or one of the guys know if you see anything unusual."

The two women hurried to the elevator and quickly made their way to their apartments with a sense of unease. Maybe Oakwood was not the safe place they had always thought it was.

CHAPTER TWO

News Travels

There is no love more sincere than the love of food.
—GEORGE BERNARD SHAW

"Good morning, Sandra," said Karen as she strolled into the library tapping her cane as she went. "I see you made it here for our meeting with Frank about the menu changes. I hope he can get here with all the snow."

The snow had continued overnight; the Oakwood campus was blanketed in it. Since the two lived in the attached apartment buildings, they had no problem getting to Oak Hall for the morning meeting.

"When I looked out and saw all this snow, I wondered if he'd make it in this early since River Road was closed last night. I guess for cooks, it's not like the postal service where the mail must go through," Sandra said with a laugh.

"As I expected, my class was cancelled, so after this meeting and my exercise class, I have a free day," Karen said smiling. "My housekeeper comes today, so

I should be able to get a lot done. It's like finding free time."

"Yes. I have several things I've been putting off, and this snow day gives me a chance to take care of some of them." Sandra was looking forward to doing whatever she liked as soon as their meeting was over.

Karen and Sandra were on the dining committee but with differing agendas. Karen was trying to promote some changes in the menu to provide healthier choices, and Sandra was intent on keeping some of her favorites such as the rich desserts and the delicious sauces the cooks created.

"We can sit and read the *New York Times* until he gets here." Karen's eyes lit up. "They always have a good section on foods and recipes, and now and then, they have a whole section on health foods. I've wanted to get our new chef to put some edamame in the succotash instead of lima beans. They have a lot of soy protein and essential amino acids, and they're low in carbs," said Karen pleased with herself.

"What on earth is edamame?" asked Sandra though she knew that would prompt Karen to get on her soapbox and give her a lecture on the benefits of so-called health foods. "Just give me good old meat and potatoes and a nice dessert and I'm happy." Karen frowned at that but resisted getting into an argument with her friend. She fluffed her newspaper and went on reading. They had known each other long enough to realize they could happily agree to disagree.

The library at Oak Hall was a beautifully appointed room with warm cherrywood shelves and cabinets, several comfortable chairs, and a few tables for spreading out papers. Local newspapers were delivered daily along with the *New York Times*, the *Wall Street Journal*, and the *Washington Post*. That day's papers had been delayed but yesterday's papers were still on the tables. Though there was no natural light in the room, the lamps and recessed lights offered good light for reading, important for residents with poor vision.

As they were paging through the *Times*, Karen said quietly, "Oh, I wanted to tell you all that my friend Mildred Fennell has just signed a contract to move in here. She's got her house on the market and is starting to get rid of all the things she's kept for too many decades."

"I don't envy her the job of downsizing," Sandra said. "I remember how tough it was for me when I sold my home and had to part with some of my treasures and mementos like letters from high school and college friends. I had the letters an old boyfriend sent me in college. Each letter had a handwritten poem. It was so romantic at the time. I missed him so much. Then at the end of the relationship, I found that he had copied all those poems out of the newspaper. So much for romance." She sighed.

"Oh, no!" replied Karen. "What a disappointment."

"Yes it was. He was tall and very good looking and was the star of the basketball team. He found someone else while I was gone. I never did have much luck with men. Maybe this dating site will change my luck."

Karen rose, grabbed her cane, and headed for the front desk. "I'm going to see if Frank's called to say whether he's coming in this morning," she softly called over her shoulder.

John, who was on duty, reported that Frank would be a little late but would try to hitch a ride on one of the road-crew trucks. Karen went to the front window and gazed out at the snow-laden trees and shrubbery. She noticed there had been no letup in the snow. The drifts had nearly obliterated the fence and sign at the bottom of the oak-lined driveway. The bushes in the yard looked like pudgy little snowmen standing still and solemn in the grey light. There was an ominous air about them.

A dark figure appeared at the bottom of the drive and made its way slowly, legs pumping high to navigate the deep, white banks that had blanketed the yard. The snowblowers had attempted to clear the areas around the main building but couldn't keep up with the large, fast-falling flakes. As the figure got closer, she saw that it was Frank even though he was bundled up against the cold. She opened the door for him. "Well, I'm glad you made it." She shut the door quickly to keep the frigid air out.

A rosy-cheeked Frank smiled faintly as he shook the snow off his cap and scarf. "It is so cold out there, and no one can get through anywhere. The plows are beginning to open portions of River Road near town, but it'll take a good while to get anyone through. The snow just keeps on coming, and they're having trouble keeping up with it. I was lucky that a salt truck picked me up and dropped me down there," he nodded toward the driveway.

"Go on into the library and I'll get you a cup of coffee. That should warm you up," Karen said. "Cream and sugar?"

"Black will be fine," he said hanging his jacket in the coatroom. "It'll take me a while to thaw out, but I'll be okay."

A few residents had drifted into the library when Karen came back with the coffee, so the three moved to a small conference room nearby.

"We haven't had a snow like this for years," said Sandra. "I can't remember the last time we had roads closed for more than a few hours."

After a few sips, Frank said, "I guess we should get started." Frank knew very little about either woman, but he knew Karen was interested in a healthier menu based on some of the comments she had made on the suggestion cards in the dining room.

"Frank, I have some ideas for menu changes I'd like to run by you to see what you think." She cast an anxious glance his way not knowing if he'd approve or not. "When talking with a few others, I've discovered that they also have concerns about our menus. We all agree the food is always delicious, but we're becoming more cautious about what we put in our mouths."

"I totally understand," he said, "and I've heard the same thing from others. There's new data out there on the special needs of seniors, and I sent a request to the administration to allow me to attend a conference in Baltimore called Healthy Eating and Gourmet Food. I expect Cathy Evans will approve it, and it should give me some ideas for improving the dining here."

"But we don't want you to take away that delicious caramel apple walnut pie," Sandra said.

Frank smiled and nodded. "No, I definitely want to provide interesting and creative options for the residents. I think we can do both. Now, getting back to your ideas for the menu," he said to Karen, "I've read some of your suggestions on the feedback cards. You mentioned using edamame in the succotash instead of lima beans. We've already planned to do that."

"How about using something like quinoa instead of rice or noodles?" suggested Karen undeterred. "There's a lot more nutrition in quinoa than in the other starches."

"But what about the taste?" Sandra asked. "Does it have any flavor?"

"If you cook it with beef or chicken broth it does," Karen said. "And what about using some wheat berries and flax seed in the soups? They're rich in nutrients, too."

"Why not add some birdseed, while you're at it?" Sandra said with a chuckle.

They laughed.

Frank said, "We'll certainly do what we can when planning menus, Mrs. Taylor. And I'll be sure to continue to include the caramel walnut apple pie, Mrs. Brown. We get a lot of positive comments about that pie, and the apples and walnuts are very healthy."

After some further give and take between Sandra and Karen, Frank stood hoping he had answered enough questions to satisfy them for the time being. "I should get to the kitchen and prep for lunch and dinner. We may not have everyone here to help because of the weather. Thanks for your suggestions, ladies," Frank said as he hurried off to the kitchen.

Unlike the residents, the snow did not give Frank a holiday. It just made his job more difficult.

Karen rose. "I have to move along to my exercise class."

"Don't forget your cane," Sandra said handing it to her. "What's this morning's class?"

"Yoga! It's nice exercise, involves every joint and muscle, and I feel so relaxed after it's over."

Sandra recalled that she had done yoga in her younger days. "Do you get down on the floor on a mat?"

"Heavens no! That was back in the good old days when we were younger. Now, we're either sitting on a straight-backed chair or standing behind it. Most of the class would have trouble getting up if we were on a mat. Sometimes when I do get down on the floor to find something I dropped, I wonder what else I can do while I'm down there," Karen said with a laugh.

As the two women were leaving the room, they were stopped by an attractive, silver-haired woman. "Have you two heard what happened yesterday?" she asked.

"No, Alice, what?" Sandra replied always ready for a little gossip.

"Well, I'm late for class, but I wanted to warn you that Elizabeth Cutler in Albemarle was robbed yesterday. The administration is keeping it quiet because they don't want the publicity, but I'm just down the hall from Elizabeth, and she was telling me all about it. She was very upset and didn't know what to do."

"Oh my gosh!" said Sandra. "The poor thing."

"Are you sure she was really robbed?" asked Karen. "Remember when Anna Brown thought she had been robbed and it turned out that she had moved her jewelry to another drawer and forgotten about it?"

"She says there's no question. She had taken her necklace and bracelet out of her safe to wear to a special party Saturday night and had laid them on her dresser when she got home. She went to put them away a few days later and discovered they were gone."

"Was her door locked?" asked Karen.

"That's part of the problem. It's not clear whether she'd locked it when she went to exercise class, but she swears she did. If not, anyone could have wandered in. Of course, the first thought is always that it could be an inside job, so Cathy's talking to some of the staff. Elizabeth is accusing her housekeeper, Augusta, of taking it and wants Cathy to call the police."

Catherine Evans had been the executive director of Oakwood since the death of her husband several years before had prompted her to leave her high-pressure job as a hospital administrator in Washington.

"Cathy is worried about the publicity, so she's hesitant to file a police report yet."

"I don't envy her," said Sandra. "A lot of people will be freaked out at the thought of a theft, and she'll have her hands full keeping everyone calm. The faster they find the jewelry the better."

"I don't think I locked my door," said Karen. "I'd better get back and check my apartment before I go to yoga." Karen and Sandra hurried off to their apartments wondering if there were more thefts to come.

Karen was shaken by the news that there may have been a robbery. She rushed to her apartment hoping she would find no unpleasant surprises. As she slipped the key into her lock, she breathed a small sigh of relief realizing that she had indeed locked her door when she had left earlier. She was a creature of habit thanks to her father's insistence on order and consistency. As a career military man, he lived what he taught his men. That had made her home seem a rather stern and cold place during her teen years, but as she grew older, she realized that her parents had set certain standards for her believing that her life would be easier and safer in the long run. She was sure they were right about that.

The news of a possible break-in was more than unsettling; it was an attack on the residents' feeling of security. Also, Elizabeth was implicating Augusta, which was shocking as Augusta was one of the best of the housekeeping staff. When others heard what a thorough job she did, they thought about requesting a change.

Not me, thought Karen. *I'm happy with Nora. She comes in and chats about everything and when she's not chatting, she's humming to herself as she cleans.* Nora was due to clean that day, so Karen decided to skip the yoga class since she was already late. She began to straighten up her apartment – empting the garbage and putting away magazines and newspapers. The crossword puzzle was not yet completed, but she decided that could wait until later when the commercials came on during her favorite TV show.

She thought about the previous night's dinner with her friends and the lovely chat by the fire as they warmed themselves. Then Sandra exploded the bomb about investigating a dating site. Karen's eyes widened at the memory of that. She hadn't believed her ears at first, but after reflecting on it, she thought it made sense for Sandra, who was still very attractive and really enjoyed male company. *Why not?*

Karen wondered why she had never considered seeking male companionship after her Dan had died. They had had a full, happy life and raised two well-adjusted children who became good citizens and self-supporting adults. But she wondered if something was missing in her advancing years. She glimpsed herself in the mirror by the door, turned, and looked at her face full on, which she rarely did. *What attracted Dan and me to each other?* She remembered that they had an instant connection when they first met, but it was more intellectual than physical. He was a rather quiet man but could easily converse about a variety of topics. As an accountant, he had been accustomed to long hours over jumbled figures, which required patience and focus, and he seemed to carry that over to his personal life. She liked that about him. She smiled as she remembered those precious times. Her musings were abruptly interrupted by a knock at the door.

"Hello, Mrs. Taylor?" chirped Nora, her housekeeper.

"Come on in," said Karen. "I wasn't sure if you would be able to get here in this weather. How are the roads now? Frank had difficulty getting here earlier."

"The plows have been down River Road, so it's at least passable but still somewhat snow-covered in spots." Nora hung her coat in the hall closet and retrieved her cleaning equipment from her cart in the hall.

"My history class has been cancelled, so I can get some things done today while you're here. I was just getting rid of some newspapers and old magazines."

"Have you heard about the robbery in this building?" Nora asked as she began scouring the kitchen sink.

"Yes, I just heard about it. I'm shocked to think that could happen in a place like this where we have such good security. I hope the jewelry turns up soon," replied Karen.

"Miss Cathy called all of us in to talk with us about it. We were all upset, especially Augusta. She's the housekeeper in that apartment you know. Evidently, Mrs. Cutler thinks Augusta must have stolen it. The housekeepers don't believe that Augusta would have done such a thing, but Mrs. Cutler seems so sure that we're all worried about Augusta." Nora was secretly relieved that it hadn't happened in one of her apartments. She didn't want any suspicion laid on her.

Ellen called Harriet just as she was finishing her after-lunch cup of coffee. "Harriet, I thought I should call you and pass on the news. Karen called me a few minutes ago from her apartment to tell me what happened. Evidently, Elizabeth Cutler's jewelry was stolen from her apartment in Albemarle. There may be nothing to worry about, but since you're more isolated in your cottage, I thought you might want to be especially careful."

"Oh dear. That is disturbing. It was kind of you to think of calling me, Ellen, but perhaps we shouldn't jump to any conclusions yet. Too many of us forget where we put things these days and spend ages looking for keys and glasses. I know I do! But even if it turns out to be a false alarm, we all need to remember to lock our doors. It can be so disconcerting when anyone can walk in unannounced."

"Yes, I remember when one of the residents in Calvert, who often got confused, entered one of the men's apartment thinking it was hers. She made his bed, tidied up the kitchen, and started ironing his shirts before he realized he had an intruder. We told him he should have locked his door. 'Hell no,' he replied. 'She's welcome anytime!'"

"I do remember that! It still makes me laugh. Luckily, no harm done that time. But let me know if you hear any more about the theft. Meanwhile, let's not worry too much about it. We may find that it never happened."

"I hope you're right," said Ellen. "Anyway, are you keeping warm in this cold weather? It looks like the snow is going to stick around for a while."

"I did get to the library to sort some books this morning. The shuttle was running, so I didn't have any trouble, but I'm not going out again. I'm getting ready for my housekeeper right now in case she can come today. You know how we always want to tidy up before they come – it feels so unfair not to play our part. Thanks for the call and the warning."

"Bye, Harriet. See you soon."

The news of the robbery was unsettling. After all, people came to a retirement community expecting a safe place to spend their later years. It was true that residents had sold or given away many of their possessions and had retained only enough to live comfortably in their apartments. However, many had kept cherished items of furniture or decoration to create a more homelike atmosphere in new surroundings. Each residence became an expression of the personality, tastes, and life story of its owner. Spacious closets had been built to allow room for clothes but also storage space for treasures such as photograph albums and souvenirs.

Some residents at Oakwood had had safes installed; they had been provided at no cost as a security measure. The last thing the administration wanted was the negative publicity of a burglary at Oakwood. Harriet had a safe installed as soon as she had found out it was available. Her jewelry meant a lot to her.

Not that she had much. Her family, who were staunch Methodists of the old school, did not smile on opulent displays. But her husband had given her some lovely pieces, and she had inherited her mother's and grandmother's rings. Harriet, ever careful, immediately locked it all in her safe and rarely took anything out.

She had found that the safe had enough room for her few important documents on its top shelf. She had it bolted to the wall behind her spare bathrobe and kept the key in the pocket of the bathrobe sure that no one would look for it there. She had told her daughter where to find it just in case.

Having put her empty coffee cup in the dishwasher, Harriet looked out the window at the river across the footpath. She decided that Augusta probably wouldn't make it in that day. After all, she wasn't as young as most of the other housekeepers and could probably use a snow day too. The weather looked so discouraging that Harriet couldn't blame her for staying home. She decided that she would get on with a few chores herself.

She had turned on the garbage disposal, so she did not hear the ring at the door. She turned around in a fright as Augusta entered the kitchen. "I tried to get your attention. I'm so sorry to have startled you, Mrs. Parker. Are you okay?"

Harriet caught her breath again. "Oh my! I'd just decided that you wouldn't come in this weather, Augusta, so I wasn't looking out for you. I should have known that the snow wouldn't stop you."

As always, Augusta was ready to tackle dust and dirt. She was fiercely diligent and regarded them as her worst enemy. Her tall, stout, physical appearance was daunting, but the residents of Oakwood had become very fond of her as she had of them. "I guess we're all a bit jumpy since the news of the burglary, Mrs. Parker."

"I'd heard there had been a theft, Augusta, but I didn't take it too seriously. We often find things we think we've lost forever. Our memories aren't always what they were. But I guess even the thought of it makes me jumpy."

"All I know is that it's being taken seriously by Mrs. Evans. She called all the housekeepers in for a meeting. She told us that Mrs. Cutler had reported that some items were taken from her dresser. She asked us to report anything we thought might be helpful but not to talk about it. I'm very distressed because I'm Mrs. Cutler's housekeeper, and she seems to think I stole her jewelry. I'm praying that the items turn up soon."

"Oh Augusta, you're the last person anyone would suspect of taking something. I'm sure the jewelry will turn up before long. Don't let it worry you," Harriet said in a comforting tone, but she wondered to herself what would happen if it weren't found. She indeed was feeling somewhat isolated in her cottage especially since Robert was away from his cottage next door. She was determined to watch for anything or anyone suspicious.

Harriet went into her bedroom to sort clothes while Augusta began to clean the kitchen. Augusta liked to clean. As the only girl in a large Irish family with six brothers, she had been mopping and scrubbing as long as she could remember. Her younger brothers had often suffered the indignity of her merciless attacks on their hands and faces with a soapy washcloth. She saw it as her duty to ensure that any member of the family was always immaculately groomed, but the boys had not suffered her efforts in silence.

She had never married in part because few men lived up to her high standards. Her one true love, as she said, had been tragically killed in a motorcycle accident when he was in his early twenties, and she had never found another who suited her as well.

With no youngsters of her own, she poured her love of children into the families she had served as a housekeeper. She still received notes and presents from those she had helped to raise, and at Christmas, she was always deluged with gifts and cards.

When she began to feel too old and arthritic to cope with the energy of young children and the messes they created, she went to work at Oakwood, where the pace was slower and more comfortable.

"I sure hope they find that jewelry soon," she said as Harriet came out of the bedroom. "I don't like feeling that some people believe I took it."

"Everyone knows how honest you are, Augusta, but I know you'll be relieved when it turns up. I bet that Elizabeth has forgotten she put it somewhere and that it'll turn up in her bedroom."

Harriet was very fond of Augusta. She liked her uncompromising attitude, which was much like her own. Harriet had also grown up with several brothers and felt that had given her a view of the world unlike that of her friends who had no brothers. She was ready to defend Augusta against any rumors or accusations; she couldn't believe anyone would think Augusta was a thief.

CHAPTER THREE
Trouble at Oakwood

There are robberies in life that leave men or women forever beggared for peace and joy.

—GEORGE ELLIOT

C atherine Evans looked around her spacious office just off the lobby in Oak Hall. She loved her office with its cool, grey walls and large window overlooking the landscape though it was covered in snow. She liked to sit at the large walnut desk and consider the activities of the coming day.

Always organized, she took real pleasure in planning ways to make life healthier and more stimulating for the residents. She had come to Oakwood ten years earlier, shortly after her husband's death, and she welcomed the relatively peaceful atmosphere after the hectic demands of her previous job as a hospital administrator. Since she had no children or close family, Oakwood had truly become her home.

convinced she would never steal from a resident, but she was the only person who had been seen near Mrs. Cutler's apartment.

Was it possible the jewelry had not been stolen at all? That she had forgotten she had moved it somewhere else? That had happened to residents before, but Elizabeth seemed so sure, and she was not known to be particularly forgetful as some of the other residents were.

Oh dear, Cathy thought. *If only Robert were here to talk to about this. I could really use his advice about now.*

She and Robert Symonds were old friends. He had been her husband's college roommate and best man at their wedding. When Robert moved to Oakwood, they had decided they did not want other residents to know of this previous relationship because of Cathy's fear that she might be accused of favoritism. They had little contact around Oakwood; instead, they occasionally met for dinner at restaurants in neighboring towns where they were not likely to be seen by anyone connected to the residence. His diplomatic background and general good sense were often very helpful when she was wrestling with an administrative problem. He had many contacts in Washington who were not available to her, and their expertise had come in very handy on more than one occasion. He could also give her feedback concerning residents' reactions to certain events or new proposals and help steer her to positive solutions.

I could use some of that feedback now, she thought as she considered her options. She was surprised by how much she missed his advice. Briefly, she wondered if she should call him. He had given her his number and urged her to contact him in Florida in case of an emergency, but she quickly dismissed the idea. She did not want to go running to Robert every time a problem arose. Perhaps she could hire a private investigator to find out what had happened without the publicity that would go with a police investigation. She quickly realized that she had no idea how to find- such a person or how much it would cost. There was no line item for "private detective" in her budget.

Cathy had already spoken to the housekeepers and security personnel and had learned that no one had seen a stranger around in the last day or two. She hesitated to call in the police since that would create a lot of anxiety among the residents. She wanted to keep things as quiet as possible and hoped to keep the newspapers from the story, but it might be impossible if an answer were not found quickly. Suddenly, the quiet of her office was interrupted by a loud rapping at the door, which was flung open before she could respond.

"Have you found out anything? Have you talked to Augusta?" A distraught Elizabeth Cutler stumbled into the room and collapsed on a nearby chair.

"Yes, I've talked to all of the housekeepers and to the security men as well. No one has seen anything suspicious in the last week," Cathy replied calmly.

"But what about Augusta? What does she say?" asked the nearly hysterical woman.

"She told me that she doesn't remember seeing the jewelry – she followed her usual routine, vacuuming the carpet and so on. She was in the bedroom for such a short time that she didn't notice anything unusual in the bedroom or the apartment."

"She must have taken it. No one else had the opportunity. No outside burglar would dare to come here in this snowstorm. I'm sure it was there when she came." Elizabeth was near tears.

"I know you're very upset," said Cathy soothingly, "but are you sure that it was there that morning? Do you think you could be mistaken and it could have disappeared earlier? This is a very serious accusation. I just can't believe Augusta is dishonest. She's been with us for several years, and there has never been a problem before."

"I'm sure it was there – I would have noticed if it weren't," replied Elizabeth defensively.

"Are you sure the jewelry couldn't have disappeared the night before? Is it possible that you didn't lock your door when you went to dinner that night?" Cathy spoke slowly and calmly hoping Elizabeth could begin to relax and think more clearly. As long as she was so upset, it was difficult to get a coherent story from her.

"I always lock my door when I leave the apartment. In fact, I remember that it stuck a little when I returned from dinner and unlocked it that night. Are you going to call the police now?"

"I'm trying to avoid that if we can," said Cathy. "May I ask if your jewelry is insured? If it is, we have no choice – it would need to be reported immediately so you can submit a claim for the loss."

"No," Elizabeth admitted sheepishly. "I kept meaning to get a separate policy for it, but I never did. I just want my jewelry back anyway – it's not the money – it's the sentimental value that's important to me."

"In that case, I'd like to hold off for a few days. If we call in the police, that will be very upsetting for the other residents. Also, it would be reported in the newspaper with your name and what was taken. I'm not sure you want that. We certainly don't want that kind of publicity for Oakwood." Cathy looked expectantly at Elizabeth.

"You might be right," Elizabeth said a little more calmly. "I really don't want my name in the newspapers."

"What about Tuesday morning before Augusta came? Are you certain you locked the door when you went to exercise class?"

"Yes. I think so. But I can't be positive because when I returned, Augusta was already there cleaning and the door was unlocked."

"So it's possible that someone might have entered before Augusta got there."

"Maybe," Elizabeth replied reluctantly, "but a stranger loitering around in the hall would have been seen. I still think it must be Augusta. I want my jewelry back. If she returns it, I won't prosecute her. I just want my beautiful necklace and bracelet back. They were a present from my grandmother Pearl, and they mean a lot to me."

Once again, she was close to tears, and Cathy felt she couldn't push her any further.

"I suggest you do a thorough search of the apartment to make sure the jewelry is really missing. In the meantime, I'll continue to question the staff and other residents who might have seen something."

"Okay, I guess I could look again," Elizabeth murmured as she rose. "But I don't think I'm going to find anything."

Cathy breathed a sigh of relief as Elizabeth stepped into the lobby. *What to do now?* She leaned on the desk, resting her head in her hands. *If only Robert were here.*

While the Tuesday Table Ladies were enjoying their snow day, some 1,100 miles south of Oakwood, Robert Symonds was sitting on a lanai, sipping coffee, and reading the *Washington Post*. Unaware of Cathy's problems, he was glad to have escaped the storm that had moved across the East Coast and had buried Oakwood. It was eighty-two with clear skies and sunshine in Florida. He should have been more excited about the great weather and lovely surroundings, but somehow, it was not as satisfying as he had expected. Well, at least he had the *Post* to read with his coffee. Some routines were inviolable.

He was very comfortable at his friends' home, which they had turned over to him shortly after he had arrived. After showing him how to use the sprinkler system for the beautifully landscaped yard as well as various kitchen gadgets, George and Joan had taken off for a month's vacation in the south of France, so he had the house all to himself. He had rented a car, which he had used to drive his friends to the airport.

"Just take us to the airport and pick us up again when we get back," George had said. "Beyond that, the house is all yours for the next month."

He had several other friends in the area and was scheduled to meet the Harrisons for cocktails and dinner at six that evening, so he did not feel abandoned. But he still felt restless, at loose ends as his grandmother used to say, as he contemplated the day that lay before him. The lack of a planned agenda was as unsettling as it was unexpected. He had already searched the bookshelves but found little of interest. Fortunately, he had brought an analysis of the current state of European politics with him, but he would have to make his way to the local library before long. For the first time, he felt a bit of envy for his friends who had progressed to reading their books electronically. The idea of carrying a hundred books with him in a small tablet or on his smartphone was suddenly very appealing even if it did not have the feel of a real book. Perhaps it was time to try the new approach. He had resisted getting a tablet and had only submitted to carrying a smartphone when his friends convinced him of its practicality.

"Bob, you can check the weather and the latest news on a phone that you carry in your pocket. You need to get with the twenty-first century," they had urged him.

So he had reluctantly given in to the new technology, but he was still resistant to an iPad or computer. He had lived all his years without them and wasn't sure he needed to start using them now. Of course, his friends pointed out that it would be much easier to write his Russian memoirs on a computer rather than his old Smith-Corona typewriter, but he liked the feel of the typewriter and was uncomfortable with the idea of starting over with a new machine.

He admitted that Sandra and Ellen put him to shame with their computer skills. Sandra had offered to scan some of his records into a computer, but he had rejected the idea. And of course his lack of email had drastically limited communication with many of his old friends – particularly those overseas – but he felt that if they really needed to contact him, they'd call. He'd given cards with his cell phone to all his friends, so they had no excuse for not calling him if they wanted. And with the smartphone, he could send and receive text messages. That was enough modern technology for the time being.

He laid his newspaper aside – he would go back to it later and clip a couple of articles he had read that pertained to countries where he had been assigned during his career with the State Department. He didn't know why he kept folders on these regions, but it was a long-established habit that he found difficult to break. Perhaps it gave him a sense of still being involved in the diplomatic world of which he had been a part for so long. That was probably why he found working on his Russian memoirs so compelling.

He set out on his morning walk intending to stroll a couple of miles down the beach and then return through the town picking up a few groceries on the way. He would be sure to stop at the fruit market. While he would select some fresh fruit shipped up from Central America, that was primarily an excuse to converse in Spanish with Jose, the owner. This was one of the best aspects of Florida – the presence of so many Spanish-speaking immigrants with whom he could maintain his language fluency. Too bad there were no Italian or Russian shop owners in the village.

He found the lack of structure in his day disturbing. At Oakwood, he had certain planned activities each day and knew for certain what he would be doing on Wednesday afternoon or Friday morning. He knew there would be lectures on Friday evenings, concerts on Wednesday nights, meetings on Tuesday afternoons, and other activities that he looked forward to. And every other week or so, there would be dinner with Cathy at one of their favorite restaurants. He was surprised at how much he missed all of that.

He had not anticipated that a month in Florida could be so dull. It had sounded quite appealing when George called to offer him their home for a month. Escape from the snow and enjoy the pleasant weather while seeing some old friends – what could be better? But he hadn't realized how much he would miss his cottage at Oakwood and his friends there. He was never at a loss for things to do at home. He spent any spare time working on his book, so he always had something interesting to do. He wished he had brought his notes with him – this was a perfect place to write. He had been concerned about bringing his typewriter and files on the plane, so he had left them in his study at Oakwood.

He wondered if the Tuesday Table Ladies had taken up his challenge to write a book. The idea of writing a mystery was intriguing. After all, it was more fun to make things up than to write nonfiction in which one had to be careful that every fact was correct and every name spelled properly. He enjoyed working on his memoirs because in the process, he was reminded of many events in his life that he had forgotten, but writing fiction was very liberating. He could spell the names however he wanted, create facts to suit himself, and perhaps most appealing, not worry about quoting other sources and footnoting statements. Since he was writing about events during his service in the diplomatic corps, he had to be especially careful not to offend those he had worked with or to reveal information that might still be classified.

He recalled a fiction-writing course he had taken in college. He had needed one more course to fill out his schedule, and since he had several particularly demanding courses in geopolitics and world history that semester, he thought that fiction writing would be a snap course. Though it hadn't been as easy as he had expected, he had liked the course and found it a happy relief from his heavier subjects. He was a bit envious of the opportunity to write a mystery novel that he had presented to the Tuesday Table Ladies. If they didn't take him up on it, he might try it himself after he finished his Russian memoirs.

In the meantime, in Florida, he had whole days looming before him with nothing planned. Was he supposed to just sit around reading every day? Perhaps he should have gone to the south of France with George and Joan. That was an area he was familiar with, and he could think of all sorts of activities he would love to do there. Florida was definitely not the French Riviera. *Maybe next year.*

CHAPTER FOUR

About Time

One of the most poignant things is unrequited love and loneliness.

—WILBUR SMITH

On a cold, grey day at Oakwood, Sandra gazed in the mirror in anxious self-appraisal. She liked what she saw. No longer the looks that had captivated the imagination if not the hearts of the men in her life, *But hey!* she thought. *Still the same face, and very few wrinkles.* The facelift had magically taken care of that. Judicious application of makeup hid her incipient brown spots. She had discovered a lovely foundation cream with retinol, rather expensive, but wasn't she worth it? She had always taken care of herself, and though those amazing whiteners young people were using did nothing for aging teeth, she knew her smile could still elicit an appropriate response. She smoothed back her hair in a gesture of self-approval.

She had never lacked for men in her life though her relationships had not always been satisfactory. Even when she was in high school, her friends would tease her and call her boy crazy. Actually, she never cared about the boys. *I guess I've always been attracted to older men, though not that much older.* Perhaps it was those well-groomed, handsome movie stars with their polished acting and impeccable manners who had stolen her teenage heart. *Where are they now?* They had disappeared from the screens.

She was seventy-six and living in a retirement community. At one time, like so many other women, she would have thought that impossible – not for her. She reminded herself that she had made the move to be equidistant from her son and daughter. They meant the world to her. They were children of a disappointing marriage, but they were all she could wish for, and she loved them dearly. She justified the idea of living at Oakwood by thinking they wouldn't worry about her and that they were not too far away. She had found out that a community for retirees was not an old people's home and certainly not a nursing home. Besides, she had discovered that after retiring from the world of work, she was lonely at home.

She found life at Oakwood pleasant enough, and to her great delight, she had made friends there. She had become especially attached to the lively Tuesday

Table Ladies. Oakwood had much to offer with access to a fitness center and exercise classes including yoga and tai chi. She knew that if she was to keep her figure, she needed a regular exercise regimen.

It had taken a while for her to get used to a world in which not everyone was fascinated by her wizardry on computers, which had been the basis of her career. There were those such as Karen who were quite content to leave that to a younger generation. *What they've missed!* she thought. She had been overjoyed to find that her friend Ellen was a computer geek much like herself. Their research on the computer had played an essential part in tracking down Laura's whereabouts when she went missing the previous year, and she was proposing to use her computer for a different sort of research. *Really,* she thought as she took stock of her present situation, *I should be grateful for my blessings.*

But there was still the fact that in the Oakwood world of married couples, many single women, and too few single men, she missed male company. None of her friends seemed to feel the same way. Perhaps it was because they had once been happily married while her marriage had been a disaster. Whatever the explanation for it, she hoped to find the companionship of an interesting man. That was what had led her to explore About Time, the dating service she had heard about.

She had tested the idea with her Tuesday Table friends. After she had explained how she was approaching it, Laura and Barbara had been supportive of the idea and Ellen was very interested; only Karen was not won over. She had not told Harriet as she assumed that she would strongly disapprove of the idea.

While others were preoccupied with the burglary, Sandra decided to move ahead with her project. *I can't believe I'm actually doing this. It's like shopping online. If you don't like it after you try it, you can send it back. Could it be that simple? Well, here goes. First, what am I searching for?*

She sat down comfortably with a large breakfast cup of Darjeeling tea. She never liked drinking tea from a mug. Coffee, yes. Tea, no. This preference had developed in her younger days in England. *Maybe he should be a tea drinker,* she mused with a wry smile. *That would be a start.*

On a more serious note, she settled down to imagine what would make for a worthwhile relationship. In her youth, good looks would have been at the top of her list, but with a deep sigh, she realized that good looks had to become a friendly face. Given her height, it would be best if he was fairly tall. Reflecting on the men she had liked best, a good sense of humor was a requirement, and a reasonably compatible background was an advantage. Her shopping list was growing.

What next? Sex appeal? No, that wasn't it any longer. What she missed most were hugs, that glorious feeling of strong arms around her making her feel safe and warm. That might be too much to ask right off the bat; she thought comfortable companionship might not allow for that. She should be practical, she thought, and look for someone financially independent. She was expecting to pay her own way, and she expected him to do the same. Finding it difficult to make up her mind about other attributes she might look for, she resolved to settle down at the computer and review the profiles of the men she had been given by About Time.

Her carefully prepared shopping list was driven out of her mind almost immediately by an instinctive reaction. One face instantly appealed to her. *Will I ever learn? I must be careful.* She had heard of con artists who were looking out for wealthy widows, but she was not at all sure she knew how to spot one. She was comfortably provided for, but she wasn't wealthy. *Probably no need to worry about that.*

She decided that she ought to be more purposeful in reviewing all the candidates keeping in mind her shopping list in case she had overlooked someone. She took her time, but in the end, she came back to her first choice. For better or worse, he seemed to be the one. Perhaps her intuition had served her well. But if she liked him, what would he think of her? Would he be anything like what she imagined?

Even for a computer expert like herself, the thought of meeting a man online was strange. *I guess it's a generational thing. The young seem to take this sort of thing for granted but it does feel like a step into the unknown.* In hopes of getting some support, she decided to call Ellen, who had not been the least bit surprised at this venture.

The phone rang several times before Ellen answered. "Oh hi, Sandra. I'm busy writing my shopping list. Time to go to the grocery store. What's up?"

"Before you leave, can you come over? Remember I showed you the online dating service I was exploring? Well, I've been on the website looking at the possibilities. You're not the only one with a shopping list. I think I've found someone. I want to know what you think of my selection. I hope you don't mind my asking."

"Oh no! I'll be right over. This is all new to me, and I'm interested in finding out how it works."

The truth was that she was even more curious to know whom Sandra had found and what he looked like.

When she arrived at Sandra's apartment, they sat down at the computer and called up the About Time site. "There he is!" exclaimed Sandra.

Ellen saw a pleasant-looking man with a thick head of white hair. There was something appealingly wistful about his expression. She took a closer look. "Sandra, do you think he has brown eyes? Hard to tell on the computer." He was casually dressed. Open collar. No tie. He looked very much at ease in the picture. Some of the other men looked self-conscious or too posed.

"I can see why you selected him. He looks okay, Sandra, but what do you know about him?"

"There's a short description that says he's six foot one. He's a widower who recently sold his financial consulting business. He plays golf for relaxation and enjoys the theater and occasional dinners out. I guess there's only one way to find out more and that is to meet him. That means I have to get back to the About Time agency to arrange it. It better be somewhere public – at a restaurant for lunch perhaps. What do you think, Ellen?"

"I'm excited for you. What do you have to lose? It doesn't matter if it doesn't work out, and if it does, who knows? And be sure to let me know how it goes. I've never known anyone our age who was willing to try this. But he does look rather nice. Are you going to tell the others about it?"

"Not until I've actually met him. There's always a chance this may not work out, and then, there wouldn't be anything worth telling."

"Keep me posted, Sandra, whatever happens. And look after yourself! I'm off to the supermarket." Ellen gave Sandra a hug and left wondering what would come of this.

It wasn't until a few days later that Sandra summoned up the courage to contact About Time. It had been a dreary weekend. She'd made no plans. The weather continued to be cold, damp, and grey. It seemed that everyone else was busy, and she herself did not attend church. She needed something to lift her out of her unusually low spirits. She had found herself often returning to the computer to see if she was still drawn to the same man. *I can't keep doing this*, she scolded herself. *I must either forget about it or take the first step. Otherwise, I'll keep wondering what I might have missed.* She reached for the computer decisively.

As soon as the arrangements were made and confirmed, she rushed to call Ellen.

"Ellen, I've done it. I've contacted About Time. And guess what? I heard right back from him. We're meeting at the Chesapeake Grill for coffee tomorrow morning. I'm excited and a bit apprehensive."

"Sandra, you're amazing. You're much more daring than I am. I feel it'll be okay. But perhaps you'd better call me as soon as you get back. What are you going to wear?"

"I don't know yet. I'll have to think about that. But I'll call you the minute I get home. You must not worry in case we decide to stay for lunch."

As it turned out, lunch was not in the cards. Sandra was back with Ellen just after noon.

"Ellen, I'm not sure how to tell you what happened. Let's go to the dining room and get a sandwich. We can sit and talk. Meanwhile, it'll give me time to settle down."

They found a quiet corner where they would not be interrupted. While they ate lunch, Ellen waited for Sandra to share her thoughts on the morning's experience. She was impatient to learn what had happened, but Sandra was in no hurry to talk.

Eventually, Sandra looked up. "There's good news and bad news. The good news is that I met such a nice man, easy to talk to and courteous. I wasn't disappointed. In fact, I was really encouraged at first. We seemed to get along so well even though we were both a bit careful not to talk about personal things or where we lived. We were both new to this online dating world. All I know is that he has a son, and he knows I have two children, but we have lots of interests in common."

Ellen wasn't about to interrupt her. It sounded promising, but there was clearly something else. What was the bad news?

Sandra continued. "He didn't seem to want to prolong our meeting. I expected him to linger because he seemed to be as comfortable as I was. I thought we were both thoroughly enjoying each other's company. Then he said he was in the middle of a big change in his life that was taking all his time and couldn't stay longer. He did say he'd like to know how to reach me when he had sorted himself out, as he put it. I didn't want to give him my phone number, so I gave him the Oakwood front office number. They can always forward the call to me. He said he couldn't give me his right now because it was likely to change. He said he looked forward to meeting up again eventually. He walked me to my car and drove away."

Ellen nodded. "Any idea what this change is about?"

"No, but my imagination has turned up a few crazy thoughts. It could be anything. Your guess is as good as mine. I think it was probably his way of letting me know he's not interested in pursuing this any further without being blunt about it. He probably knows that it hurts to be turned down. The trouble is, Ellen, that I liked him a lot, and I feel really disappointed. Maybe it wasn't such a good idea after all. I think I should forget about the whole thing. I expected and hoped for too much. Now, I feel let down."

"Only time will tell, Sandra. Let's not tell the others about this. In the meantime, we have to decide whether we want to try writing a mystery story. That should take your mind off this. There's a lot to look forward to here."

Sandra was to learn how right Ellen was.

CHAPTER FIVE

Creative Dining

Creativity takes courage.

—HENRI MATISSE

Frank was busy at his computer lining up menus for the following month. The weather was beginning to thaw, so he was researching dishes that felt like spring. *I think that spring's finally on its way and that it's time to refresh the menu*, he thought happily. This was a chance for him to show his kitchen creativity. Up to that point, he had felt somewhat constrained by the menus planned by the previous chef who had been at Oakwood for several years. He had tried to dress the old menus up a little, but they still seemed tired and dated to him. He had been there for a few months at that point, and he felt freer to offer more-exciting choices to the residents. Of course, salads were always a favorite, but he wanted to include something new – maybe dandelion or beet greens that were not only colorful but nutritious as well.

Lamb was always a springtime favorite, but it could be prepared in new and different ways. Desserts were adaptable to any season, and while ice cream and sundaes were favorites, he knew he could offer other, more-exciting desserts. He smiled as he thought of Sandra and her expression of delight for the caramel apple walnut pie with a scoop of vanilla ice cream of course.

He knew Cathy was planning to open up the dining room to the outside – on the patio overlooking the river. That meant they would be serving meals al fresco, which would provide many opportunities for his creativity. He could think of a dozen dishes that would be suitable for eating outside. The residents of Oakwood had been very generous with their compliments for the food he prepared, but he knew he could do better given the chance. And this was his chance. At the same time, he was conflicted when making choices between what was fresh and creative and what was healthier for this population of active but elderly people. In his months at Oakwood, he had grown fond of the residents. He strove to help them live the longest, healthiest lives possible and still give them dishes they would consider gourmet offerings. It was a fine line to contemplate at times. Just as he clicked the save button, Kevin walked into his office.

"Hey Frank," he said. "What's new with you?"

"Great news, Kevin. They've approved my trip to the conference," he replied waving the approval letter for the seminar on Healthy Eating and Gourmet Food at Johns Hopkins hospital. "I should get a lot of ideas for more-interesting and creative dishes. There are so many things I've been wanting to try."

"That's great," Kevin said.

"I have some real aspirations for dining at Oakwood, and I'm hoping this seminar will give me some solid ideas," Frank said. "It seems to me that healthy eating is an important aspect of living longer, but it doesn't get the attention it deserves. I'd love to develop a TV show maybe called *Cooking for the Vintage Generation* that incorporates healthy eating with creative gourmet foods. It would be great publicity for Oakwood as well as a real public service."

"That's a wonderful idea, Frank. Have you talked to Cathy about it?"

"Yes, and she's very supportive. I see this seminar as a foundation for my plan, and that's part of the reason she approved my going."

"I understand the Tuesday Table Ladies are thinking about writing a book. That's something you could do too especially if the TV show gets off the ground. How about *Cooking at Oakwood*?" Kevin asked excitedly. "But what about a replacement chef while you're gone?"

"I'm working on that," Frank said.

It wouldn't be easy to get someone to come in and take over while he was away. There were people who could do the job because they were retired or between assignments, but there was no guarantee they would follow his directions. Chefs liked to show their flair for unique cuisine whenever they had the opportunity. Frank wanted to allow his substitute some latitude as far as that was concerned as long as it didn't upset the residents.

"I have some leads I hope will bring the right person here in my absence. I know anyone who comes won't be able to duplicate my recipes exactly, but they should be close to what the residents expect."

Frank always tasted his food as he prepared it. He knew exactly what was missing or what was needed to make it the best. It could be a small pat of butter at the end of making a sauce or a dash of garlic powder in the gravy just before serving. Every chef had his or her own secret ingredients.

"I guess you'll draw up a set of instructions before you leave, right?" Kevin asked. "You know, I could be a lot of help while you're away. Just let me know what I can do and I'll be on it," he said with a smile.

"I have confidence in you Kevin, and of course, I'll count on you to help things run smoothly while I'm gone."

He and Kevin had become good friends in the time Frank had been at Oakwood, and he knew he could depend on Kevin in his absence.

"You know, I've mastered your version of tiramisu, so if you have it on the menu, it'll be as if you were in the kitchen," Kevin said laughing.

"You rascal you!" Frank said with a chuckle. "You've been spying on me."

They laughed heartily as Kevin left to set up the tables in the Riverview dining room.

Frank moved into the kitchen and scurried around to begin the preparation for seared tilapia with lemon caper sauce. Of all the protein sources, seafood was his first love. It had to be fresh, and it had to be prepared to order. You couldn't cook a big batch of fish and reheat it because that tended to give it a rubbery, tasteless quality. Even lemon and capers couldn't bring that back to life.

The servers began to arrive and prepare menus and water glasses. Sprigs of fresh flowers sat in the center of each table. The flatware was enfolded in light-blue napkins and ready to be set out at each place. The dining room had a festive feel to it partly because of the light reflecting off the river outside. It made the glasses sparkle though they were empty. It was a beautiful sight to behold as Frank surveyed it.

He was indeed a lucky man to be working there. He nodded in satisfaction.

As Kevin and the other servers prepped the table settings, the Tuesday Table Ladies were gathering at their usual table.

"I can't believe it's March already," Ellen muttered as she took her seat. "It's beginning to feel that spring may come after all."

"Yes, the weeks seem to go by faster and faster," Karen said. "I think it's because we're so busy."

"Or because we're so old," Harriet said with a smile. "Time often seemed to drag by when we were young. And especially just before holidays or birthdays."

"You may be right, Harriet," Ellen said as she picked up a menu. "Oh there you are," she added as Laura and Barbara joined them.

"It's still cold out there, but I saw some crocuses peeking out of the ground this morning, so there's hope that spring's almost here," Barbara said rubbing her hands. "Sandra's on her way. We just passed her in the Oak Hall lobby. She said she'd catch up shortly."

Sandra burst into the dining room, hung up her coat, and made her way to the table. "Sorry I'm late. I was getting the latest news from Elizabeth's friend Alice. Apparently, Elizabeth is still claiming that Augusta took her jewelry. She thinks Cathy waited too long before she called the police, and that's why

Augusta wasn't arrested. Of course, Cathy did bring in the police after it became clear that the jewelry was not going to turn up, but that didn't satisfy Elizabeth."

"That sounds like Elizabeth. She can be really stubborn when she gets an idea in her head," Barbara remarked.

"I'm sure Augusta wasn't arrested because she didn't steal anything. Elizabeth just can't face the fact that she's misplaced them," Harriet said gruffly. "I heard that there were simply no leads the police could go on, and the only reason to suspect Augusta was that she had cleaned the apartment. That's hardly enough to arrest someone."

Emily appeared with water, and the group turned their attention to the menu. The night's entrées of seared tilapia and chicken piccata were both appealing, so it took some time for the women to make their choices. They all opted for the Caesar salad with extra anchovies as listed in the menu, so no one headed for the salad bar.

"I think it's awful for Elizabeth to go around accusing Augusta like that," Ellen said angrily. "Especially since there's no evidence to support her accusation."

"Yes, after this, some people will always think Augusta did something wrong even if there's no evidence she did," Barbara said. "Some residents have even asked to change housekeepers."

"That's so unfair," Ellen said. "Isn't there anything we can do?"

"Let's just hope it all dies down. People will find something else to gossip about and forget about Elizabeth's jewelry," Laura said. "Thank goodness we haven't had another robbery. That would have really freaked people out."

Emily came with the salads, and the conversation came to a temporary halt as they turned to the food.

"I see the chef is putting edamame in the salad now. I bet that's your doing, Karen," said Sandra with a mischievous smile.

"Well, it certainly makes the salad more nutritious," Karen replied. "Besides, it tastes good. It adds some crunch to the greens."

"Have you all given any further thought to the idea that we should try to write a mystery?" Ellen asked. "Robert should be back soon, and we want to have something to tell him. Maybe we could write a story about someone who experiences a computer scam."

"I don't think that's suspenseful enough. A good mystery needs at least one dead body," Barbara asserted.

"Two dead bodies would be even better," said Laura laughing.

"Sure, serial killers are the most suspenseful. You never know who'll be killed next," Sandra added.

At that point, the laughter from the Tuesday Table had grown so loud that it was attracting the attention of the other diners.

Emily finished serving the entrées, and the table became quiet again. Those who were facing the window looked out at the gradually greying sky. The banks of the river were dotted with the last remains of the previous month's snowstorm – bits of white here and there. The river was empty, too cold even for the hardiest sailors and other boaters. Most of the boats had been winterized, covered for the season, and tied up at their docks or stored onshore until spring officially arrived. The river still held a few icy patches that floated downstream with the current. It was a pleasant view even without the sailboats that would soon be lazily tacking up and down the river.

Sandra broke the silence. "Seriously, I think it would be a lot of fun to write a mystery together. We're not too old to try something new, and I bet we'd learn a lot doing it."

"I know," exclaimed Karen. "We can write a book about a woman who uses an online dating service, and you can do the research!"

"Yeah," added Harriet. "She starts dating this really attractive, mysterious man, and then she gets murdered, and he's the suspect."

"Or even better – he gets killed and she's the suspect. I don't like it that the woman's always the victim," Barbara suggested laughing.

"Yeah, I like that idea," Laura said.

"Well, we can't decide on the crime before we have our characters laid out," Sandra said.

Sandra was very uncomfortable with the direction the conversation was taking. She was still smarting from her experience with online dating and didn't want to think about it at that point. She was surprised at how hurt she had been by her date's rebuff. Only Ellen was aware of her unhappy experience at the Chesapeake Grill. She hadn't connected with another profile. *Maybe online dating isn't all that great after all*, she thought.

"It seems we should each write a character and bring it to dinner next week. That would give us a chance to see if we can actually write something," Sandra said.

"But what's the setting?" Karen asked. "Where would our mystery take place?"

"How about on an African safari?" Ellen asked. "That would give us a mysterious atmosphere to work with."

"But none of us has ever been to Africa. I don't think we could write very convincingly about it," Barbara replied.

"Or Tahiti? It would be a lot of fun to write about Tahiti," Ellen said excitedly.

"Have you been to Tahiti?" Harriet asked sharply.

"No, but I've been to Hawaii, and it's similar – a Pacific island. We could read up on it, and I could research it on the internet."

"How about Paris? Paris is always fun and romantic, and a couple of us have been there, so we could probably write about it," Sandra said.

"They always tell authors to write about what they know," Barbara said thoughtfully. "Maybe we should write about a retirement community. We all certainly know about that."

"Yes," replied Laura. "It's the one thing we all have in common."

"Well that's the most sensible idea yet," Harriet said.

Emily appeared to clear the table and take orders for desserts and coffee. The night's special desserts – a warm cherry sundae or a French silk pie were chosen by everyone except Karen who opted for "Just decaf coffee please."

As they waited for dessert, Barbara turned to Sandra. "How's the online dating experiment going? Have you found anyone interesting yet?"

"Well," Sandra replied reluctantly. "There's one guy whose profile sort of stood out from the others, and I met him very briefly, but it didn't work out. I don't know if I'll try it again. I wasn't going to say anything to you all unless I actually connected with someone I might see again," she said looking nervously at Harriet.

"Why didn't it work out with the guy you met?" Karen asked in awe that Sandra had really carried through with her objective of meeting a man online. "How did you arrange a meeting?" "How old is he?" "Where does he live?" Her tablemates' questions rained down on Sandra too fast for her to answer. She was becoming upset with the questioning. She did not want to talk about her date and how he had rejected her. That was exactly why she hadn't wanted to say anything until she had seen someone a couple of times and was ready to introduce him to the group. Fortunately, Harriet was silent.

"The arrangements were made through the dating service, and we just met for coffee. I don't think we'll see each other again. Ellen saw his profile."

"I thought he looked very distinguished. He's about our age, and according to his profile, he has some interests in common with Sandra – theater and things like that. I'm surprised it didn't work out, but you never know."

Emily arrived with desserts and coffee saving Sandra from further interrogation. However, the

Tuesday Table Ladies were not likely to let the matter end so easily.

Eager to change the subject, Sandra turned back to Robert's proposal that they write a book. "So what do you all think? Should we try writing up some ideas for our mystery story?"

"I suppose we could each write a description of one character and see how it goes," said Karen slowly. "We certainly have plenty of material to draw on," she added, looking around the room.

"I think we have to be careful not to draw too heavily from our neighbors here at Oakwood," Barbara said. "That could cause a lot of hard feelings or even a lawsuit or two."

"I can think of a few characters I knew before I came here who might be good fodder for a novel," Karen said smiling.

"Oh, me too," Ellen chimed in. "I think it would be fun to try."

"I think that before we get to the characters, we need to talk about a plot," Laura said. "Why don't we each write a brief proposal suggesting a scenario for our mystery and then see if there's one we can agree on?"

"You're probably right, Laura. I guess we do need at least the outlines of a story before we tackle the characters," Sandra said.

So the six women decided somewhat reluctantly to try to put something on paper before the next Tuesday dinner. Even Harriet agreed to go along with the group. As an ardent reader, she was curious to see if she could write fiction. This was a far cry from the numerous reports she had written for various committees or the grant proposals she had prepared to support her favorite community programs over the years.

Intrigued with the ideas that had started to form, the women quietly donned their coats and headed across the short passage to Oak Hall. They were lost in plots for a mystery written by the Tuesday Table Ladies. Was it really possible?

CHAPTER SIX

Another Robbery?

*I beg you take courage: the brave soul can
mend even disaster.*
—CATHERINE THE GREAT

C athy put down the receiver with a sigh of relief. *So Robert's coming back. He even sounded as if he was looking forward to it.* She had missed him during the month he had been in Florida. She wasn't surprised he was ready to return. She could not imagine him being content to sit on the beach watching the tides roll in and out. True, he had left to escape the worst of the winter weather, but the snow had disappeared. *He experienced a lot worse during those Russian winters,* she thought.

Even all those years ago, she had realized he was not one to sit still for long. She had wondered how he would adjust to life at Oakwood after he moved in. His eventful life in the Foreign Service must have been full of contrasts and challenges. At least in Florida, he could look forward every day to a round of cocktails and dinners with old friends and former colleagues who had retired there. But he was there on his own for the rest of the day. She had sometimes wondered why he had never married. His career seemed to have taken over his life. Gary had once mentioned there had been a special woman in Robert's life, but he had never said any more than that, and Robert had never alluded to her.

As her husband's closest friend, he had been best man at their wedding. He had always visited them when he came home between assignments overseas. They had been delighted by the tales of his adventures and were affectionately amused by the development of his more sophisticated tastes of which his mother's British racing green Jaguar was an early herald. Life at Oakwood would be so different. She was sure that its proximity to Washington was the compelling reason for his decision to move there. It had been the hub of his career, and there were still many contacts for him there. She smiled, recalling that in his usual charming and tactful way, he had told her that the fact she was its executive director had convinced him Oakwood was the place for him.

Occasionally, he was called to Washington to consult on international and personnel issues. Even at Oakwood, he could be useful. The Tuesday Table

Ladies had put him to work when they were alarmed at Laura Lambert's disappearance the previous year. She wryly reminded herself that she had missed him when Elizabeth Cutler's jewelry was reported missing. Even so, Oakwood was hardly the center of high-level intrigue.

She was sure he would return wearing the nicely bronzed tan one acquires casually in the shade of the deck while reading. She wondered what it might be like to be sitting on that lanai with Robert. *I'm jealous,* she thought thinking of her days that were preoccupied with the well-being of her charges at Oakwood. What with the Cutler robbery, the chef taking off for a seminar, and the extra worries of the snowstorm, she had been exceptionally pressed. However, she had to admit that the snow had been a dramatic and exciting event and would be talked about for years to come. Robert had missed out on that one.

She wanted to make sure his cottage was ready for him. She checked the housekeeping staff's assignments and was pleased that Augusta was the one who normally cleaned his cottage. Poor Augusta was having a miserable time with the report of the theft from the Cutler apartment, and she was no longer assigned to clean there. Asking her to get Robert's cottage ready for him would be a signal of confidence in her.

She called the housekeeping manager to arrange for Augusta to freshen up Robert's cottage before his return. She found herself worrying about other things such as whether his car would start or if there was food in the cottage, but she knew it wouldn't be appropriate to fuss about things like that. At Oakwood, he was a resident and not supposed to be a close friend.

Augusta was happy to hear the news that Mr. Symonds was returning. She liked looking after his cottage. Everything was in good order there, and he had such interesting things. He had lived in places she would never have known even existed. He must have read all those books with titles that sounded like movies. She was always careful not to disturb anything in his study. He still did a lot of work. She knew it was important because the papers often had government headings and seals. Sometimes the envelopes had "Urgent" in large letters written on them. He had told her he was writing a book about life in Russia.

She arranged for extra time for this job as he had been away for a month, enough time for cobwebs to grow. It would be easy enough to propel her cleaning wagon down the path to his cottage since the snow had gone and it wasn't raining. She was in a cheerful mood. The days were getting longer, and the snowdrops were beginning to break through the flower beds. She had decided that she must stop worrying about the missing jewelry or what Mrs. Cutler thought. Even if it were eventually found, she still had a feeling Mrs. Cutler would feel she was responsible for its turning up where it was not supposed to. Just the same, she wished they would find out what had happened to it.

She made sure she had everything she would need at the cottage. It would be such a nuisance to have to go back to the main building for supplies as the cottage was in a row facing the river and separate from Oak Hall. It was so quiet there. The only sounds came from occasional boats passing along the river. Mrs. Parker lived in the cottage next door, and she would never cause a disturbance.

It wasn't until she unlocked the door that she realized all was not well. She saw marks on the floor of the hallway as if someone in snow-covered boots had been there. The snow had melted and dried leaving blurred marks in a trail into the living room.

Someone had indeed been in there. She instinctively knew that no one from Oakwood would have left such a mess had they attended to anything in the cottage. She stopped abruptly at the doorway but

dismissed the thought that there might still be someone in there. The marks were not new. But someone
had definitely been in the cottage. Still bruised from
the accusations of the jewelry theft, she assessed the
situation carefully. *I think I'd better find Mrs. Evans.*
She carefully closed and locked the door. Leaving her
cleaning wagon outside the door, she marched down
the path to the main building where she prayed she
would find Mrs. Evans. She was in luck. Mrs. Evans
was in her office and free to see Augusta.

Cathy noted Augusta's anxious face as she came in
and closed the door. Something had upset her again.

"Sit down, Augusta. What's wrong?"

Augusta took a deep breath. "Oh Mrs. Evans, I
think you should come and have a look and tell me
if I should go ahead. I guess I'm nervous after what
happened with Mrs. Cutler, but I didn't like what I
saw. Mr. Symonds would never have left his cottage
like that."

Cathy walked to her office closet for her coat.
"Let's go back together. You have the key. We'll take
another look and then we'll know what to do. Don't
worry. You certainly did the right thing in coming to
me right away. I assume you haven't told anyone else."

Augusta nodded in wordless confirmation. She
was relieved to know Mrs. Evans understood how she
felt.

They walked in silence to the cottage, each wondering what they would find. Augusta unlocked the door, and Cathy stepped inside. "Wait there, Augusta, while I investigate." She was careful to walk around the markings on the entrance floor and made her way into the living room. She was horrified to see there that drawers had been pulled open and rifled through. Books had been pulled off the shelves and were lying in tumbled piles on the carpet. She turned to Robert's office and to her dismay saw that it had been torn apart with drawers open and folders and papers strewn over the floor. She hastily retreated to the entrance in a state of shock. She paused for a moment to gather herself. *Poor Robert. What a sight will greet him!*

"What should I do, Mrs. Evans?" Augusta asked. "Shall I go ahead and clean the hallway?" She knew that those snowy footsteps spelled trouble but was not aware of the mess in the living room and den.

Cathy collected her thoughts. "It would be best if we left things as they are until Mr. Symonds comes back. He's due tomorrow. He can decide what needs to be done. I'll ask you to go ahead with the cleaning when he's ready. Meanwhile, we'll lock the door and keep this to ourselves. No point in stirring up worries when there may be no cause for that."

Augusta was relieved. Mr. Symonds would know what to do. She marshalled her cart and started down the path to her next job oblivious to the actual conditions inside the cottage.

Cathy in contrast was worried. She realized this matter was very different from the disappearance of Mrs. Cutler's jewelry though it might be tempting to connect the two. *Who would turn Robert's cottage inside out? What were they looking for? Thank heavens he's coming back soon.*

Back in her office, Cathy took stock of the situation. She wondered if she shouldn't wait for his arrival to do something. Normally, she would have immediately called in the police, but this was not a recent robbery. The residue of the footprints was evidence of that. Waiting one more day would surely not make a difference. Robert would be able to make a better assessment of the situation before the police arrived since he was totally familiar with the contents of the cottage. He would know whether anything had been taken before the police had disturbed the site. It did seem the wisest course to wait for his return.

She decided to meet him at the airport. She would gently break the news of what was awaiting him at his cottage on the drive back. She had arranged for one of the drivers to take him to Reagan airport and meet him on his return. She asked the receptionist to have the driver call her. When he did, she would arrange to go in his place armed with the flight number and time of arrival.

She dreaded the thought of it. *Poor Robert. What a homecoming awaits him tomorrow!*

CHAPTER SEVEN

The Absent Chef

A good cook is like a sorcerer who dispenses happiness.

—ELSA SCHIAPARELLI

That evening, Harriet was in her usual chair and looking out the window at the river flowing slowly toward the bay and recalling the happy hours she had spent racing her sailboat on these waters as a teenager. She looked down at the one-page document she had typed earlier. It wasn't as good as she had hoped – thinking up a scenario for a mystery novel wasn't as easy as it had sounded when Laura proposed it at dinner the previous week. Apparently, years of writing reports and reading mystery stories hadn't been enough to make her a writer. Her musings were interrupted by Sandra, who arrived with her usual burst of energy. She was determined that no one would suspect she had been depressed by her dating misadventure. She hoped the mystery writing would give her something cheerful to think about.

"Hi, Harriet. Did you write up some ideas for our mystery? It looks like you have some notes there."

"Well, I have something on paper, but I certainly hope you and the others have some better ideas than I came up with," Harriet replied gloomily.

"I'm sure that among the six of us something worthwhile will emerge," Sandra said enthusiastically. "I think this is going to be a lot of fun."

"I'm still not convinced that it's feasible, but I'm open to giving it a try." Harriet looked at her notes and sighed.

Barbara and Laura came in and took seats.

"Well, did everyone write something? It took me longer than I thought it would," said Barbara pulling some pages from her bag along with a bottle of Pinot Grigio. "I'm ready for a glass of wine. I think what I wrote will sound better with wine."

"I think you're right," said Harriet.

"Right about what?" Ellen asked as she pulled up a chair to the table.

"Drinking to enhance our literary abilities," replied Sandra with a smile.

"What literary abilities?" asked Karen as she joined the group. "After all these years of writing my columns, I've discovered I have absolutely no talent for fiction. Apparently, I have no imagination. I can write only about concrete subjects such as food and household tips."

"That's no problem, Karen. We'll just put lots of food in our book and you can write those parts." Sandra's enthusiasm was not easily diminished.

Emily passed out menus and water and wine glasses, and the group soon turned to the important topic of the moment – which would be better, the sweet-and-sour pork or the prime rib? Decisions made, dinner orders given to Emily, and wine glasses filled, the conversation turned back to their attempt to create a scenario for their mystery novel.

"Who'll go first?" asked Laura. "I have to confess, like Karen, I don't have anything. I started to write a story about one of the residents in a retirement community who disappears and her friends go looking for her. After an hour or so, I decided I couldn't write about something so close to home, and I gave up. I kept obsessing about it and couldn't come up with any other plots. Why don't you start, Sandra? This was all your idea."

"Okay," Sandra said nodding as she put a couple of sheets of paper on the table. "I picked up on Ellen's idea about an online dating service since I have some limited experience in that anyway." She looked at the others hoping they wouldn't expect her to explain her online dating experiment any further. It was still a painful memory, and she wondered why she had ever decided to try writing a scenario on the topic. Perhaps because she was still preoccupied with her unhappy experience.

She went on. "My heroine, Samantha, finds a really attractive man online, Henri. He's French, but he lives in Washington, DC and is very romantic. She has a great time dating him. He takes her out to dinner and to concerts and plays. She falls for him, but when she finds out he's married, they have a big fight in public. Then he's found murdered, and Samantha quickly becomes the leading suspect. So she and her friends must find the real killer to prove her innocence. That sends them to several places like bars and social clubs where they've never been before, and it leads to several interesting adventures before they finally discover his wife was the murderer."

"I kind of like that idea. Would we use a retirement community as the setting?" asked Barbara.

"We could, but it wouldn't have to be."

"Since he's French, it could be a very sexy story. That would be fun to write," Ellen said expectantly. "I don't think a publisher would want it or anyone would read it if it didn't have a lot of sex."

"Speak for yourself, Ellen. I read a lot of nonfiction that doesn't have any sex at all," Barbara retorted.

"How's he killed?" asked Harriet, always the practical one.

"I think it should be a bloody, vengeful death – a stabbing or something," said Sandra.

"Blood and sex. Sounds like a winner," Ellen said with a laugh.

"I think it has some real possibilities, but let's hear what some of the others have come up with," Laura suggested. "How about you, Ellen?"

"Well, I took my inspiration from the stories about computer hacking that have been in all the news lately."

Ellen's scenario was interrupted by Emily, who appeared with the soups and salads. No one had chosen to go to the salad bar, opting instead for the chef's special marinated vegetable salad, which was always very popular. Barbara and Ellen had ordered the French onion soup as well as the salad.

"Ooh, what's wrong with the salad?" asked Ellen grimacing as she spoke.

"I think it's the dressing. It's much too sour – not at all like the dressing we usually get with this dish. I always order it because the dressing is good," Barbara said putting her fork down in disgust.

"You're right, the dressing is too sour. And the vegetables are a little soggy too," Laura added.

"It's certainly not up to the standard we've come to expect from Frank," Harriet said.

"Yes, I'm very disappointed," Karen remarked.

Those who had ordered soup pushed aside the salads and started on their soups. "This is okay," Barbara said.

"Yes, but where's the melted cheese that should be on top?" asked Ellen.

Emily came to the table. "Is everything okay? Can I get you anything else?"

"Yes, I'd like a fruit cup. This salad is too sour. I just can't eat it," Harriet replied.

"I'm sorry. We've had a lot of complaints about the salad tonight. Frank is away at a conference for a few days, and he hired a substitute to fill in. The salad dressing is Frank's special recipe, and the temporary chef was trying to guess how he made it."

Karen, Sandra, and Barbara requested fruit cups to replace the discarded salad while Ellen and Laura went to the salad bar.

"I wonder where Frank's conference is." Karen said. "I hope it's somewhere warm."

"I hope he's not interviewing for a chef position somewhere else," Sandra said. "I'm afraid we might lose him. He's so good."

Ellen and Laura returned with large salad bowls, and Ellen remarked, "The salad bar was jammed.

Evidently, we weren't the only ones who didn't like tonight's vegetable salad."

"I'm not surprised," said Harriet. "It was almost inedible."

"Well, I guess we shouldn't complain too much – the food is usually so good," Laura pointed out. "It must have been really hard to find someone to fill in for Frank."

"Okay, Ellen. You were going to tell us about your scenario," Laura said.

"Well, all the warnings about computer security set me thinking about what could happen to a woman who was a victim of computer hacking, but I couldn't decide whether she should be the victim or the murderer. I finally decided that someone whose computer was frozen, identity stolen, and bank account emptied might well be angry enough to kill if she could find who'd done it. That's where I got stuck. How could the victim track down the hacker especially with her computer out of commission? Do you all have any ideas?"

"Your idea's interesting, but I'm going to object to making a woman the victim again. That just feeds the common stereotype of woman as victim," Laura pointed out.

"But if she turns out to be the murderer, she'd be the aggressor as well as the victim," Karen responded.

"However, both scenarios so far make the woman vulnerable to an internet scam – one to an online dating scam or an identity theft," Laura protested. "Stories like that reinforce women's fears of computers."

"That's the STEM gap – it's not just computers. It's math and science in general," Barbara pointed out.

Ellen responded. "I used to try to think of ways of getting my female students more interested in computers. In most cases, if I could get the girls to try them out, they soon became converts. Of course, now, our grandchildren start with computers in kindergarten or first grade, and there's not the same problem that we had when I first started teaching computer science in high school."

"Well, we aren't going to solve that problem here. Let's get on with our plot proposals or we'll be here all night," Harriet said. "I'd like some more wine, please."

As the wine was being passed around, Emily removed the soup and salad bowls "Dinner will be out in just a minute," she said cheerfully.

"Okay, Barbara. What do you have?" Laura asked after Emily left.

"Someone mentioned writing about what we know, so what I know best is the law," Barbara replied. "However, I'm no John Grisham. I don't know how he comes up with all those stories."

"We aren't professional novelists. We're just trying to see if we can do this for fun. If it turns out it's not fun, we'll just drop the whole thing," Sandra said. "Go on, tell us what you have."

"Okay, here goes." Barbara took a deep breath before reading her short paragraph. "Nancy is a retired lawyer living in a retirement community like Oakwood. One day, she's approached by Carol, another resident, who asks to speak to her about a private matter. It seems she's being threatened with a lawsuit by a former employee. Carol had owned a small shop, and one of her former clerks is now accusing her of sexual harassment back when he was working for her. It's a ridiculous charge, but he promises to drag her through the mud with outrageous publicity. He has a cousin who runs a tabloid newspaper and is ready to run a front-page story. He wants $100,000 to stop the story and keep quiet. Nancy, who's still licensed to practice law, agrees to take the case and advises Carol not to pay him any money. A short time later, the employee is found dead, and suspicion falls on Carol after the cousin goes to the police with the story. Eventually, the murderer is identified as another victim of the dead man's scam and Carol is cleared."

"I think that's great," Sandra said enthusiastically.

"It certainly has a lot of possibilities, but I have to point out that we have another female victim," said Laura.

"But the dead person is a man," Ellen pointed out. "He's the real victim."

"You all know what I mean. Poor elderly lady gets scammed by a man. At least her lawyer is a woman," Laura replied.

"The killer could be another woman. That would even things up a bit," Karen suggested.

"Yes. That would help show that all women are not so helpless," Laura said." Let's hear what Harriet's come up with."

"You'll be happy to know that my victim is a man and that the women are strong and decisive," Harriet said.

"Somehow, I'm not surprised Harriet wants to write about strong women," Barbara said in an aside to Laura.

"Go on, Harriet," Laura said.

Before Harriet could begin, Emily returned with their dinners; the table became very quiet as they started eating.

"The prime rib is a little overdone, but it's okay," Barbara said.

"Yes, the substitute chef should be able to manage a prime rib without ruining it, and the sweet-and-sour pork is edible, but it doesn't have Frank's special touch. He always does something with the sauce that transforms it. This is rather mundane," Karen remarked.

The six women ate in silence until Emily returned to clear the table and take orders for dessert and coffee. Tonight, there was everyone's favorite – tiramisu – and even Karen ordered dessert. As Emily was carrying away the plates on a large tray, Laura turned to Harriet. "Okay now, what do you have, Harriet?"

Harriet took a large sip of wine and began. "My heroine is the chair of an education committee at a retirement community. She's invited a well-known professor from Washington, DC to appear on a Friday night in January. When they get an unexpectedly heavy snow that day, she's concerned that he might cancel, but he assures her by phone that he'd be there in plenty of time. He was going to leave the university with time to spare." She stopped for another sip of wine.

"When he fails to show up before the lecture and he doesn't answer his cell phone, she has to inform the large audience that the talk is cancelled and she'll try to reschedule. She assumes he's been trapped somewhere on the freeway, and she decides to wait in the lobby for a while in case he makes it there after all. She's chatting with the clerk on duty at the desk when a security guard rushes in to call the police. He's just found a man's body covered in blood in a car parked just outside the entrance. It's her missing lecturer, and feeling responsible for bringing him there, she sets out to uncover the murderer. She enlists some of her friends, and they eventually find the killer. I haven't figured out the details of why he was killed or how they solve the mystery."

"Wow, Harriet. I really like that. It's very believable, and I like it that the women solve the murder," Sandra said excitedly.

"Me too," said Laura as Emily returned with desserts and coffee.

"Well, the tiramisu is delicious as always," Karen said after tentatively trying it.

"You're right," said Ellen. "This chef seems to be good with desserts."

"Maybe Chef Frank made the tiramisu before he left," Laura suggested unaware of Kevin's newly acquired talent in the kitchen.

"What shall we do now about our mystery story? Are we ready to decide which scenario to go with, or do we want to write some others first?" Sandra asked.

"Or do we want to undertake this at all?" asked Harriet. "I'm still not convinced we can follow through properly, and we don't want to make fools of ourselves trying to do something we just aren't equipped to do."

"Oh, I definitely think we should continue and see where it goes. Remember, we're doing this for fun, so let's not get too serious." Ellen was eager to explore the possibilities of this enterprise.

"Besides, I'd like to show Robert that we can write a book too. We should think about it during the week and decide what to do next Tuesday. There are some really good ideas in tonight's plots, and I think we should explore them further," said Sandra with her usual enthusiasm. "After all, they're always telling us how important it is to exercise our brains, and writing a mystery would certainly do that!"

"You're right. This is one of the most interesting brain exercises we could undertake," Karen said.

They agreed to postpone a decision on the plot of their mystery until the next week. They also agreed that in the meantime, if anyone wanted to write a new scenario or add to one of those already proposed, she could work on it. They weren't convinced they could actually follow through writing an entire book, but they were ready to give it a try.

CHAPTER EIGHT

Welcome Home

---

*Most of American life consists of driving
somewhere and then returning home, wondering
why the hell you went.*

—JOHN UPDIKE

Robert returned his rental car with the satisfying thought that he would soon be back driving his own car again. The car he had rented boasted every amenity available. Not being accustomed to them, he had enjoyed finding out how they all worked, but he found he scarcely used them in Florida. The exception was the rearview camera that was so helpful in backing the car. Yes, the GPS guided him to his friends' houses but no more effectively than did the Garmin GPS he kept at hand in his old Jaguar. No new car with all its innovations could replace the feeling of getting behind the wheel of that artifact of another, more-elegant age.

The flight back was mercifully uneventful but with the same inconveniences – cramped seating and coffee that tasted of dust. He reminded himself of the days when he had traveled to Europe on the Concorde. It too had cramped seating, but that had been more than compensated for by the elegance of the service and the speed of travel.

But he was retired and no longer had the privilege of business class travel. So for three hours, his tall frame was subjected to the confined torture of his aisle seat. At his stage of life, it seemed the ultimate indignity especially when paired with the restless fidgeting of the passenger in the next seat. *Next time I will pay the extra dollars for a seat with more legroom. It would be well worth it.*

Grateful to be back on land, he made his way down the endless airport passageways and followed the signs to the baggage area. The passageways seemed to grow longer with every airport expansion. *Or am I just growing older?* He dismissed the thought with a shudder. As his had been a direct flight, he was confident he would eventually meet up with his suitcases. Meanwhile, he would look out for the Oakwood driver. It would be good to be home again. He was looking forward to working on the lecture on contemporary diplomacy he had been invited to give at the Fletcher

School at Tufts University. It was also time to get back to his book about his time in Russia.

It was not that the stay in Florida had not been a welcome break. The house his friends had lent him was well appointed with every comfort. There was a shaded deck on which to enjoy the welcome warmth of the sun. He had mercifully escaped the snowstorms he had heard had blanketed Oakwood. He enjoyed the good conversations each night with friends and colleagues from his years in the world of diplomacy and intrigue in which he had thrived. How very different from life at Oakwood. Except for the mystery of Laura's disappearance last year, daily life had settled into a comfortable routine broken only by his consulting visits to the State Department in Washington. Even those were becoming less frequent. On the other hand, he would at last have time to spend on his writing.

There was a delay while a seemingly endless parade of luggage tumbled out of the fast-moving luggage belt. He stepped back to allow the anxious seizure of suitcases by travelers in a hurry and almost fell into Cathy's arms. "What in the world? Cathy!" He was startled at this unexpected but pleasant encounter.

"Welcome back, Robert. I hope you had a good trip. I'm here to drive you back to Oakwood instead of the driver. I'll wait here until you get your luggage."

All that was said in her best cheerful way. Deep down, she was dreading having to tell him why she was the one who had come to meet him. His looking so healthy and relaxed after his month away made it even harder.

His bags arrived, and he followed Cathy out of the terminal and into the short-term parking garage. They stowed the luggage in the trunk and headed to Oakwood.

"I knew you wouldn't have had time for lunch. You must be hungry," she said. "I haven't had any myself, and it's past my lunch hour. I suggest we stop on the way and get a bite to eat, okay?" She did not want to tell him what was waiting for him at home while she was driving.

"Good idea. That'll save me from having to de-frost something." Robert was not an enthusiast when it came to the likes of Lean Cuisine.

Cathy pulled into a small Italian restaurant she had seen on the way to the airport. She thought it looked like a quiet, unhurried sort of place, which is what she needed for breaking the bad news to Robert. When they had ordered, she wasted no time.

"All's well at Oakwood, but I have to tell you that's not the case with your cottage. I'm so sorry, Robert, but someone broke in and ransacked it."

Robert looked incredulous. "At Oakwood? Are you sure?" He paused. "Has anything been stolen?"

"I don't know. Here's why."

She went into all the details – what had led up to her going in and what she had seen there the day before. There was no way of softening the blow. Robert was clearly stunned as he listened.

When she finished, he asked the obvious question: "Have you called the police?"

She explained that the police had already been there on a fruitless search for the solution to Mrs. Cutler's missing jewelry. She added that in his case, she had decided to await his return before making any move. "I thought you should decide what was best once you'd seen the situation for yourself. Waiting one day more wasn't going to make any difference. And it is your home."

Robert was relieved. He was used to being in control in difficult situations, and he thought it imperative to assess what might be missing before taking any action. *Was this a burglary or something else?*

They ate quietly and promptly paid the bill. The rest of the journey seemed interminable, but at last, they turned into the Oakwood driveway and headed straight for Robert's cottage. They arrived without interruption. Without taking the luggage out of the trunk, he opened the front door. He saw the footprints on the front hall just as Cathy had described them. Robert took note of them before entering the living room and his office.

The sight of the chaos in his office concerned Robert the most. The legacy of his life's work was in those files, and more important, the papers he had recently been working on. They were strewn all over the floor. *What prompted this? Was a burglar looking for money or stock certificates?* It was impossible to tell at that stage whether anything had been stolen or broken. No ordinary burglar would have been so thorough in going through the files, the contents of which were scattered all over the carpet. The intruder had ransacked the living room, where there were some valuable items, but that was to be expected of a burglar. He was not sure why his file cabinets had been so thoroughly pawed through.

Given the nature of his connection to the State Department, he knew this needed to be reported to the authorities. Not that he had kept highly secret papers or even confidential ones. He badly wanted to start to clean up the mess, but he knew he had a duty to alert the proper people first.

"Cathy, I need to use the phone before I do anything else, and I don't want to call from here. May I use one of the guest rooms for tonight? I won't even leave my luggage here. I have enough Florida gear in the trunk."

"I'll arrange for the nearest guest room right away," Cathy said reaching for her cell phone. Dreading his answer, she added, "Are you going to call the police?"

Safely ensconced in the guest room, Robert settled down to make his first phone call. He quickly got through to his contact at the State Department. When anything unusual happened, it was expected that one would inform the relevant officer. He explained carefully who he was and why he had called. "I cannot tell at this point whether this is a simple burglary. It might be that, but the obvious fact that someone thought it important to go through my professional files suggests the possibility that there's more to it than that."

The officer took careful notes and promised to call him right back.

Robert unpacked a few necessities as he waited for a return call and instructions. It was not long before one of the senior officers, Colin Odoma, whom he knew quite well, called back. "Sorry to hear about this, Robert. I take it you're all right?"

community had something to do with that too. *You cannot give up on life here!* He simply had to wait.

A gentle knock on his door roused him from the armchair in which he had collapsed after his phone call. He cautiously opened the door. It was Cathy.

"I've brought you an early dinner. I felt sure you wouldn't want to appear in the dining room just yet."

"You read my mind. I should eat something. It might turn out to be a long night."

The guest room was well supplied with a microwave and some utensils. He sat down at a small table while Cathy organized the meal – vegetable soup, a hearty beef stew, and some freshly baked rolls.

Cathy was curious to know what had been the outcome of his phone calls, but she waited patiently while he had a chance to enjoy his soup. "Now tell me what's happening, Robert."

He dabbed his mouth with his napkin and looked at her. She was a mixture of a capable commanding presence that could lead you into battle and gentle concern he could describe only as feminine. He smiled.

He told her what was about to happen – a crew was on its way and would arrive well after it was dark. They would call him as they approached, and he would meet them to lead them on the pathway around the outside of the buildings to his cottage.

They were unlikely to meet anyone walking there on a cold night. They could be relied on to be efficient, and they would likely be away well before morning. "Perhaps I'll even have time to get a little sleep," he said cheerfully not wanting to alarm her any more than necessary.

"That's all very well, but it still leaves you with a real mess to clean up," she replied. "And what if you find that things have been stolen?"

"No use looking too far ahead, Cathy," he said trying to reassure her. "I haven't any idea what I might find or not find. I left no cash there, and other things of value are so unusual that they'd be hard to get rid of. As for my papers, it's hard to imagine anyone would think a retired foreign-service officer would have anything of consequence. Now for that good bowl of stew!"

The men came just before midnight. They went silently and efficiently through their routines and left the cottage almost as they had found it. Robert waited patiently throughout their search for evidence still wondering what the new day would bring.

He had seen the agents off the Oakwood grounds using the circuitous route by which they had come. Lights had been on in some windows where a few residents were probably watching late-night television, and the usual pathways were illuminated, but their route had been in total darkness; no one could have seen them come and go. They had worked in silence, taking pictures and dusting for fingerprints. It was probably a fruitless endeavor; whoever had broken in had undoubtedly worn gloves. Only the prints in the hall might come in useful, but that was a long shot at best. He was exhausted and relieved to see the agents leave. He was ready to return to the guest room and collapse on the bed.

Dawn found Robert fully dressed and fast asleep on the guest-room bed. He awoke when Cathy called to say that she was bringing him breakfast before the rest of the community began the day. He unpacked some fresh clothes and his shaving kit, and he took a hot shower. He knew he had a very long day ahead of him.

The best thing about breakfast was the strong coffee. Cathy had brought him fresh bagels, cream cheese, and orange juice. After that, he was ready to face the day. Cathy reluctantly left him; she had her own responsibilities.

"I'll catch up with you later, Robert. Good luck. I know you have quite a job ahead today."

"Thanks a lot for everything, Cathy. You've been wonderful. Now, I must carry on and work my way through this."

He made his way back to his cottage encountering only some of the staff who were arriving early for work. The day was beginning for them too.

His cottage looked as it always had on the outside. A few green spears of snowdrops were beginning to show themselves – early harbingers of spring. He paused before he opened the front door; the memory of the upheaval inside was fresh in his mind. Steeling himself, he unlocked the door and stepped into the hallway. The footprints were still there, but since the men had gathered the evidence, he would wait for Augusta and her mop and brushes to clean them up later.

He started on the living room. He was anxious to find out what might have been stolen. He was worried about his papers, but he wanted to find out whether there were indications the intruder might have been a common thief looking for valuables. He did have a few pieces of Bolivian silver of Inca design he would have hated to lose. Some of his personal treasures were farewell gifts presented to him by his colleagues or members of the diplomatic corps in countries where he had worked. They were usually engraved or fastened with metal labels indicating their origin, surely of sentimental value to him only.

He began with clearing the floor so he could move around more easily without stepping on his possessions. He set about the task methodically, carefully putting items back where they belonged. Nothing seemed to have been broken. "Well, that was a start."

Soon, the living room began to look more like his home, and his spirits rose. He resumed his task with renewed energy. A few minutes later, he was startled by a knock at the front door. He hoped it was Cathy. He opened the door and was surprised to see Harriet, his next-door neighbor. With his usual presence of mind, he greeted her before she could say a word.

"Good morning, Harriet. As you see, I'm just back from vacation. It's good to see you. But I can't ask you in as I'm busy sorting things out after being away. Perhaps you could come back later?"

"Oh yes, Robert. I'm sorry to interrupt you, but I just came over to check. I thought I might have seen a light in here late last night when I got up to have a drink. But I was half-asleep and forgot you were supposed to be away. So when I woke up this morning, I thought I'd better make sure everything was all right. I'm relieved to find you here. I hope you had a good time in Florida. It's good to see you back. I'm on my way after lunch to meet Laura and Barbara to talk about the mystery story you challenged us to write. We must get you to join us at dinner so we can catch up. I'll see you later."

"Thank you, Harriet. I'll look forward to that." He knew she would quickly spread the word that he was back. He had better get to work again.

It was painstaking labor, but so far, he had found nothing missing. He was glad he didn't live in a large house. He was optimistic that at this rate, at least the living room would soon be back to normal. The bedroom was relatively undisturbed. Whoever had been there had obviously focused on just two rooms. Judging by the extent of the mess, his den was going to prove the greater challenge

That proved to be the case. Papers and documents had to be gathered off the floor where they had been thrown, sorted out, and replaced in their files or folders. He began by making separate piles by subject, which would then have to be sorted again. He made a path to his desk where the drawers were hanging open, most of the contents having been discarded on the carpet. He paused to try to envisage what he had kept in the various drawers. Fortunately, he had always been very orderly in his work, so he had a fairly good idea of where everything was supposed to be. For a moment, he pictured his gun at the back of the drawer of the small chest where he had stowed it after cleaning it. Then he recalled distinctly that he had put it away in the locked box in his closet before leaving for Florida. He quickly investigated.

Well, that's one thing to be reported as missing, he said clenching his jaw in anger. He had kept the gun when he moved in as he was uncertain whether he still might face an occasion when it would prove useful. It was registered in his name, so it was traceable if found. *Small chance of that,* he thought with a deep sense of frustration wondering what else was in store for him.

With renewed urgency, he went back to the job of going through his papers and restoring all the items he usually kept in his desk. It was tedious work. At another time, it could have been enjoyable to sort through the papers, news clippings, and notes he had accumulated over his career. Under the pressure of the circumstances, it seemed almost insulting to treat his life story that way. But there was no alternative; he had to keep going until he was certain nothing else was amiss or missing.

Cathy arrived with soup and sandwiches for lunch, and after that, he worked through the day. It was not until the end, when he had put his files and folders back in order, that he realized there was something he had not found. He checked again just to be certain in case he had misfiled it. It was the aging materials he had accumulated when he was stationed in Moscow years earlier. He was puzzled. He knew he hadn't tossed them out. They had all been there among the other folders stored in chronological order. He had occasionally added to the file when he came across pertinent articles, and he had been referring to it frequently as he began writing his Russian memoirs. In fact, he had been of two minds as to whether to take it with him to Florida. He wished he had done so. The loss was painful.

He would have to report to his contact in Washington but not before he tried to recall what he might have put in the folder, certainly not any classified or sensitive documents. He had collected items more in the nature of memorabilia. Surely no one but he would have been interested in those.

He picked up the phone to make his report about the missing gun and folder. It had been a distressing day, and he was ready to start putting all this behind him. He wanted to return to his routine and sleep in his own room.

He didn't know there was still more to come.

CHAPTER NINE

Mysteries

The first page sells that book. The last page sells your next book.

—MICKEY SPILLANE

Laura and Barbara left the dining room after a light lunch and took seats in the Oakwood lobby. "Apparently, Elizabeth is still claiming Augusta must have taken her jewelry, and she's very frustrated that the police have done nothing," Barbara said. "In the meantime, a lot of residents are frightened that a thief is lurking around every corner and that they're going to be attacked any minute. It's very unsettling. I hope they figure out what happened soon."

"I agree with Harriet that the jewelry will probably turn up in a drawer someday, and I'm annoyed at Elizabeth for making all these charges against Augusta. I'm afraid it wasn't stolen at all and she's gotten everyone upset for nothing," Laura said. "If there actually is a thief on campus, her accusations about Augusta only confuse the situation and make it harder to discover who's really responsible."

"When Harriet gets here, we can go into one of the conference rooms near the library to work on her scenario for our mystery. I'm glad we narrowed our choices down to the two ideas – Harriet's murder of the guest speaker and Sandra's scenario about online dating," Barbara said thoughtfully. "We can work them out in more detail and then chose which one to pursue."

"Yes, me too. I liked your idea of the female lawyer, but by choosing Harriet's scenario to work on, we'll get her involved, and I think it's important everyone participates," Laura said.

"Sandra told me that she, Karen, and Ellen were meeting this afternoon to work on Sandra's idea. I'm curious to see what they come up with. I think they're all going online to research the dating scenario. I bet they'll have fun with that."

"As far as I'm concerned, that's the whole idea. If it's not fun, we should quit right now, right?" Laura replied.

"I'm curious to see if we can actually do it. The idea of writing a mystery is rather intimidating, but it's better than talking about our aches and pains over dinner."

"Or gossiping about our neighbors," Laura said with a laugh. "Or listening to people bragging about their grandchildren."

"I'm sorry to keep you waiting," Harriet said as she hurried up to them. "I was helping someone find a book, and I hated to leave the library until we found it. Have you been waiting long?"

"No," said Barbara. "We had lunch and were waiting for you, but we've been here only a few minutes."

"Do you two want to talk here or in a conference room?" asked Laura.

"Why don't we just sit here? There's no one else in the lobby now, and these chairs are so comfortable," said Harriet. "I'm glad they still have the fire going even though it's warmed up some. It makes such a cozy atmosphere."

"You're right," said Laura. "Why don't you pull up that chair and join us. I have a notebook and pen to take notes, but I see this as more of a brainstorming session."

Harriet moved a chair closer to the two women and pulled a small notepad from her pocket. Barbara also pulled out a pen and paper.

"Where should we start?" asked Barbara. "With the setting or the characters?"

"I think with the characters," Laura replied. "Harriet has proposed that the story take place in a retirement community, and that's enough for now. We can fill in the details of the setting later."

"I agree." Harriet nodded. "We need to get a handle on the characters first."

"Okay then," said Barbara. "What do we have so far?"

Over the next hour, the three women discussed the characters Harriet had outlined and began to describe them in more detail. They also talked about the retirement community in which their story would take place and decided to locate it in Florida, a favorite place for retirees.

"I think that's enough for now. We should probably write up what we have and bring it to dinner next week," suggested Barbara.

"Why don't I draft an initial document and circulate it to you two for editing before we show it to the others?" Laura asked.

"That's an excellent idea," Harriet replied. "I like what we have so far. I'm still not sure we can pull this off, but it should be fun trying."

"One other thing. We don't have a name for the main character. We need to come up with an appropriate name for her," Laura said.

"I think Harriet should name her. It's her story," said Barbara.

"Oh no," Harriet objected. "This is a collaboration. It belongs to everyone, so we all have equal voices."

"You're right, Harriet. We don't want any competition or hard feelings if our ideas aren't used," Laura responded. "Why don't we each come up with a name, and we can pick one next time we meet."

"That sounds good. I'm off to the art studio. I'm working on a painting that I hope to finish this afternoon," Barbara said. "It's a birthday present for my granddaughter, and I need to get it in the mail in the next few days."

"I'm sure she'll love it. You're so talented," Laura said. "I'm going back to my apartment and type this up while it's fresh in my mind," she said waving her notebook.

"I have to go back to the library and finish some paperwork," Harriet said. "I need to order some supplies and a couple of new books. By the way, I saw Robert today."

"I knew he was due back soon, but I haven't seen him yet," Laura replied. "When did he get back?"

"I guess he got home yesterday. I thought I saw a light in his cottage last night, but until I saw him this morning, I decided I must have been mistaken. That happened once before – a few weeks ago. The window in my bathroom faces the side of his cottage, and I thought I saw a light in his window, but I decided later it must have been a reflection from the streetlight out front. He didn't ask about the book, but I told him we were working on it. I don't think we're ready to tell him any more until we have a better idea of what we're doing."

Laura rose and gathering her pen and notebook. "Have you heard anything else about the cybersecurity warning that Cathy circulated? It sounded serious – I certainly don't want to be the victim of a ransomware attack."

"Yes, I understand the Donaldsons were affected. They hired some IT guy to come in and clean their computer. Apparently, it was a real mess," Barbara said solemnly.

"Oh boy. That's all we need," sighed Harriet. "It's hard enough to keep up with the changing technology without adding problems like that. Well, I'm off. See you all later." She walked over to the hall leading to the library as Barbara headed for the art studio and Laura strolled toward her apartment building.

Laura was thinking about the report she had volunteered to write when she almost bumped into Robert. "Hey, we were just talking about you. Harriet said she'd seen you. When did you get in?" she asked.

"Oh," he said in surprise. "I got back yesterday, but I haven't seen many residents yet."

"You must have dinner with us on Tuesday and tell us all about your Florida trip," Laura said smiling.

"Okay, it's a deal," Robert responded. He headed toward the front door to get the shuttle back to his cottage.

While the three women were working on their scenario about a missing speaker, Sandra opened her apartment door to admit Ellen, who was carrying her laptop.

"Karen's not here yet, but you can set up next to my computer on the desk. I think there's room for them both. Karen won't have a computer."

"No, she's adamant about that. It's too bad. I think she misses a lot by not being online," Ellen said.

"I've been googling online dating sites to see what's available," said Sandra as she followed Ellen into the second bedroom, which served as a guest room and office.

"This should be fun," replied Ellen setting her laptop on the desk next to Sandra's. "We want a site for

young adults – our heroine is too young for About
Time."

"That depends on what we decide," said Sandra.
"We did say it could take place in a retirement community like Oakwood. Let's see what Karen thinks."

As if on cue, they heard a knock followed by,
"Hello there. Shall I come on in?"

"Yes please. Ellen just got here," Sandra said.

Karen came into the room pulling a notebook and
pen from a canvas bag. "I'm not sure what we're doing. As I said, I'm more used to writing helpful hints
than mystery novels." She sat in a comfortable chair
near the desk.

"So how should we start?" asked Ellen.

"That's a good question," replied Sandra. "My scenario was pretty sketchy – I didn't give a lot of details."

"I think we need to talk about the setting and the
characters," Karen said. "When you described the
scenario at dinner, you didn't indicate where the story
takes place."

"You're right. We need to decide that first. Ellen
and I were just talking about whether it takes place
in a retirement community or a setting for younger
people."

"I think the characters should be younger and
especially if the guy's French," Ellen proposed

enthusiastically. "It'll be a lot sexier if they're younger than residents of a retirement community."

"I think the story could be sort of sexy even if it's set in a retirement community. There are lots of seniors on About Time. Besides, the focus of the story is on the mystery, not on sex." Sandra scrolled through a list of online dating sites.

"Yes, we have a few romantic stories here at Oakwood," Karen said somewhat wistfully.

"Regardless of her age, what else do we know about Samantha?" asked Ellen. "Is she divorced, widowed, or never married? Apparently, she's interested in dating, but that doesn't narrow it down very much."

"And what about this Frenchman? Henri, you called him. What's he doing in Washington? Does he live there permanently, or is he there on an assignment of some kind?" Karen asked.

"The one thing we know is that the characters are using an online dating site," Sandra pointed out. "Why don't we start there and look at a few sites. They may give us some ideas. We can go to sites for younger people as well as About Time."

"Why don't you bring one of the chairs over so you can see the computer screen," Sandra said as she pulled up one of the sites she had explored before.

"The whole idea of meeting people online seems so weird," said Karen as she sat next to Sandra. The desktop had a large screen that all three women could see.

"I know my grandson is dating a woman he met online," replied Sandra. "It's very common among the millennials." Sandra did not mention her own upsetting experience but could not help thinking about it. She hoped the others wouldn't bring it up.

"In fact, my son married someone he met online, and she's a wonderful daughter-in-law," added Ellen.

"It's hard to know where to start," said Sandra. "There are over nine hundred sites now, and they're all slightly different. Some of the most frequented ones have over fifty million people who have signed up at one time or another."

"Good heavens! I had no idea they were so widespread," Karen responded in shock.

"I was looking at some of the more popular ones before you came. Several of them require you to take a personality test up-front so they can match you with appropriate contacts. Others let you browse the portraits. I found a site that doesn't require payment until you're ready to contact one of the matches. I thought if we filled out a personality test for Samantha, it might help us flesh her out a little more."

"That's a good idea!" Ellen said. "We'll have to make some decisions about what she's like to answer the questions in the test. Let's try it. We can go through one with a younger character and then do one with an older character on About Time or a similar site for older people."

She and Karen watched closely as Sandra brought up the website for one of the dating services. "How old is she?" asked Sandra as she began to answer the questions posed on the website. They slowly worked through the form making up answers for their imaginary Samantha. They occasionally stopped to discuss an answer, but gradually, a psychological picture of their character began to emerge.

"This is the strangest research I've ever done," Karen observed wryly. "But I have to admit it's kinda fun."

"I think it's exciting. It makes me want to fill one out myself," Ellen said. "Now they want a picture. I don't think any of us can pass for our twenty-eight-year-old Samantha. What are we going to do?"

"I thought about that. I have a photo of myself at about that age," Sandra replied. "I'll scan it into the computer and attach it to our form. Since we're never going to meet any of the guys they suggest, it doesn't matter what we use. We just want to get an idea of how Samantha would go about this process so we can write about it."

"I'm really impressed with what you can do on the computer, Sandra. I'm beginning to think that maybe I've been missing something by not having one." Karen sighed.

"It's never too late, Karen," Sandra said smiling. "I'd be glad to help if you decided to move into the electronic age, but you wouldn't need a computer. A tablet or even a smartphone would probably be all you need."

"I'm going to give it some serious thought," Karen said. "I just might try it. My kids have been nagging me for years, and they've threatened to give me an iPad for Christmas, but I talked them out of it."

The women spent another hour on several websites studying the portraits of the young and middle-aged men and the descriptions of their interests and personalities. There were a few oohs and aahs as Sandra scrolled through the possible matches for Samantha.

"I wish I were about forty years younger," Ellen said as an especially handsome man's picture appeared on the screen. "I'm sorry they didn't have something like online dating when I was their age. But of course by then, I was married."

"They didn't even have computers when you were their age," Karen pointed out.

Sandra finally moved on to a website for those over sixty. "I already have an account on About Time, so we can look at some of the men they want to match me with, but I think Samantha should also try one of the other sites for seniors."

After looking at some of the possible matches for Sandra on About Time, the women selected another senior site to explore.

"Whose photo shall we use for this site?" asked Ellen.

"Since I have no intention of ever going on it myself, you're welcome to use mine if you like," Karen said.

"Great!" said Sandra. "Hold still. I'll take a photo with my phone and download it."

The site also had a personality test, and again, they answered the questions but that time as an older Samantha.

"You were right, Sandra. Answering the questions for Samantha does help us think through who she is," Karen said.

"Too bad we can't do the same for Henri, but reading the descriptions and comments of some of the guys gives us an idea of what he might be like," said Ellen as Sandra began to scroll through some of the men matched to their fictional Samantha.

"This one looks like a hoodlum," Ellen said pointing to the next portrait that filled the screen.

"I like this one," Sandra said as another photo appeared. "He resembles a guy I used to date. He was really hot if you can use that term to describe a seventy-year-old professor," she said with a laugh.

When they decided they had done enough research, they moved into the living room to discuss their findings over a glass of wine.

"So after visiting the sites, what do we think the setting should be? A retirement community with older characters or a younger setting?" Sandra asked.

"I'm still not sure that a romance between seniors would be passionate enough to lead to a murder," Ellen pointed out.

"I vote for the retirement setting," Karen said. "I think it would be easier to write about something we're all familiar with especially since we haven't written anything like this before."

"I still like the idea of writing about a thirty-something woman involved in online dating, but you might be right that we should stick to what we know since this is our first novel," Ellen said. "What do you think, Sandra?"

"Let's try writing up the scenario with the older characters. If that doesn't work, we'll rewrite it with a younger Samantha and Henri. Of course we could try it with a younger woman and older man. That might work."

"Or an older woman and younger man. I like that even better," Ellen said laughing.

The three women began hammering out a scenario for their proposed novel to present to the other Tuesday Table Ladies.

CHAPTER TEN
Robert's Discovery

Whatever happens in a house – robbery or murder – it doesn't matter. You must have your breakfast.
—WILKIE COLLINS

Robert awoke the next morning in his own bed. He felt content to be back in his home. Then he remembered the shock of the alarming events of the previous day. The disarray the intruder had left his cottage in had been bad enough, but then there was the loss of his gun and the apparent theft of one of his files. His contact in Washington had not indicated that he thought the theft significant. In the context of world events, Robert too would have judged the event insignificant, but he had done his duty and reported it because in that world, anything out of the ordinary was considered worthy of note. On reflection, he decided to give some thought to the possible contents of the missing file again after breakfast. It was going to be more challenging to complete his book without all those items, which served so well to prompt his memory.

Dressed and shaved, he walked over to the dining room where a simple breakfast of muffins and fruit was available with some coffee. He was warmly greeted by staff and the residents who were early risers as he was, but conversation was usually subdued at that hour. Most of the residents had become accustomed to getting their own breakfasts at a more leisurely pace.

The best part of his breakfast was the coffee. Armed with a second cup, he returned to the cottage, where he settled down to think about the missing file. At every posting, he had kept a file in which he collected miscellaneous items that had interested him or which he judged might turn out to be useful in the future. They were often news clippings, photographs, and programs. That meant most of it turned out to be professionally unproductive, but he had found that they served as great reminders of his foreign postings. He had kept them when he retired as great *aide memoires.* He was angry that the Russian file had disappeared since he was using the contents for his book.

He could not say that he had enjoyed his assignment in Moscow, but he did not regret the experience. More than any other, it had demanded constant vigilance and the ever-present awareness of being under surveillance. He had not developed any friendships there as he had in other places though he had a genuine admiration for the fortitude of the Russian people. The file included profiles of people and places that had interested him. There was no point in dwelling on it; he needed to put it behind him. He had other things to do including dinner next Tuesday to hear about the Tuesday Table Ladies' progress in writing their mystery.

Later that morning, Cathy called. "I wondered if I could pick up lunch for two and come by at about one to see how things stand at the cottage."

He was delighted he had to admit. It was not just the thought of lunch but also the prospect of time with Cathy. Always good company, she was the thread that wove its way through the past to his earliest days. She and Gary had always been in America, where he could depend on a warm and reviving welcome. Gary, his jovial and loyal friend since their Harvard days, had Cathy always by his side. It was Cathy, who had been on her own since Gary's untimely death, upon whom he had continued to rely. She had changed so little over the years that he had taken it for granted she would always be there, always the same. She was he had to admit a compelling reason he had chosen to retire at Oakwood.

The cottage was reasonably tidy. He drew out a small table, expanded its leaves, and placed a chair at each end. He found his placemats with scenes of Holland he had bought in the Hague, two tall water glasses, and some cutlery. He had an hour to fill before she arrived, so he set about renewing delivery of his newspapers and journals. His accumulated mail would be delivered that day as he had instructed. He called the main desk to tell the staff that he had returned. After lunch, he would wander down to the in-house mailbox to see what awaited him there. There would be the usual listing of the week's events, new staff appointments, and miscellaneous announcements. Having done all that, he would begin to feel he had never been away. He settled in his favorite chair to wait for Cathy and lunch.

Cathy had a busy morning. No, an unusually busy morning. Every morning was a busy one. But that day, one of the gardeners who kept the grounds so well had cut himself badly while clearing a tree that had fallen in the recent snowstorm. She had waited with him until an ambulance arrived to take him to the hospital. And a cook in the Oak Hall dining room had lost his temper when a supplier was very late delivering vegetables that had been scheduled for dinner that evening. She knew he was somewhat temperamental, but he was very good at his job, and the residents appreciated him, so time spent calming him down was time well spent.

She also secured a promise from the company that they would deliver as expected in the future. They could always find a new supplier, but a talented cook was another matter. So she was relieved when the crises were over and life returned to normalcy and she could look forward to her lunch break.

She was surprised to find Robert's cottage looking as if nothing had ever happened with one exception – the hallway footprints still needed a thorough cleaning. Robert greeted her with a cheerful smile.

"Robert, you've worked wonders here. You've certainly earned your lunch!"

She had been harboring the thought that he might decide when this was all over to move from Oakwood to one of several attractive retirement communities in the Washington area. He might even join his friends in Florida. That was a depressing prospect. She was very fond of him; he was her link to so many happy times in the past when Gary was alive.

She placed her lunch boxes on the kitchen sideboard and turned around to give him a lingering hug, which he generously responded to.

They ate lunch in an uncharacteristic, self-conscious silence. Finally, Cathy asked whether he thought there would be any repercussions from the break-in.

"I can't imagine what they'd be, Cathy. I'm convinced I should forget about it now and just get on with life. I've done all I needed to do about it."

"Does that mean you plan to stay on in the cottage?" Her tone suggested that she was almost afraid to hear his answer.

He looked at her thoughtfully. His answer came slowly. "I hadn't even thought of leaving. You know, I'm beginning to think you and I need each other now."

"In that case, dear Robert," Cathy replied with a happy smile, "I'll ask Augusta to clean your cottage first thing tomorrow morning."

CHAPTER ELEVEN

Disturbing News

---

*One must never set up a murder. They must
happen unexpectedly as in life.*
—ALFRED HITCHCOCK

Harriet as usual was already seated at the table on Tuesday evening when the Tuesday Table Ladies gathered for dinner. Sandra and Ellen hung their coats and scarves in the coatroom before going to the table.

"Brrr! It still doesn't feel very spring-like," said Ellen as she sat.

"At least it's not raining or snowing," Sandra said as she pulled out a chair. "I see there's an extra chair tonight. Do you know who's coming?"

"No. Emily just said Laura called and told her to set an extra place tonight," Harriet replied.

"Hello everybody," Barbara said smiling as she sat.

She was quickly joined by Karen, who had followed her into the Riverview dining room. "Who's joining us tonight?" she asked looking at the extra chair.

Before anyone could answer, Laura appeared at the table with Robert in tow.

"Look whom I managed to convince to have dinner with us tonight," Laura announced happily. "Now we can hear all about his adventures in Florida."

"It didn't take much convincing, and I'm afraid I didn't have many adventures in Florida," Robert said. "In fact, there always seems to be more going on here than anywhere else. Compared to Oakwood, I found Florida to be rather dull."

Emily approached the table with menus and water glasses.

"Is Frank back yet, Emily?" asked Ellen. "We sure miss his cooking."

"No, but Cathy Evans said he'll be back soon," Emily replied. "Does anyone want anything besides water to drink?"

"Yes. We'd like some wine glasses please, and would you ask them to open this bottle in the kitchen?" Sandra said as she passed a Pinot Grigio to Emily.

"So what did you do all that time in Florida?" asked Laura. "Did you spend a lot of time on the beach?" She could not picture Robert sitting in a beach chair watching the tide come in.

"No, I'm afraid I spent most of my time on my lanai reading and waiting for dinner. I have quite a few friends in the area, and almost every night involved some social activity or other. I will say that it was good to meet up with old friends and very relaxing as well. But other than that, there just wasn't much to do. What's been going on here?"

"You didn't miss too much," Barbara replied, "but we did have a mystery. Elizabeth Cutler's jewelry went missing, and she accused Augusta of taking it."

"Cathy mentioned the theft, but I didn't realize Augusta was a suspect." Robert was surprised. "Augusta is the most honest person I know. Elizabeth must be mistaken."

"You're absolutely right," agreed Harriet. "I've said all along that Elizabeth has probably misplaced it and it'll turn up eventually."

"Apparently, the police agreed since they interviewed Augusta and a number of other staff and residents, but they didn't find anything," Laura said.

"Also, Frank, the chef, is away, so the food just hasn't been the same," Sandra said.

"No," added Karen. "His replacement and the kitchen staff have tried their best, but they just don't have his talent for sauces and spices. I'm glad they brought in a temporary chef, but I certainly hope Frank gets back soon."

"The food has been disappointing," Ellen chimed in petulantly. "It's usually so outstanding that we all look forward to dinner, but lately, it's been more institutional. I can't wait for him to return."

The conversation was interrupted when Emily returned to take their orders and handed the opened wine bottle to Sandra, who filled her glass before passing the bottle.

As soon as Emily left with their orders, Sandra raised her glass. "Here's to your return, Robert. We're glad to have you back."

"Yes, here's to Robert. Salud!" They all raised their glasses of wine or water, and Robert smiled as he thought how glad he was to be back at Oakwood.

Robert joined four of the women at the salad bar. Once they were seated again and Emily had served soup to those who had ordered it, Robert turned to the others.

"Cathy told me a little about this robbery you mentioned. When did it happen?" Robert asked.

"It was soon after you left," Karen replied. "We think Elizabeth may have just misplaced her jewelry, but it hasn't turned up yet, and some of the residents are very upset at the idea there may be a thief on the campus."

"I think Elizabeth may be the only one who's totally convinced she was robbed," Barbara said. "But she's so sure someone got into her apartment and stole her necklace that a lot of other residents are really scared she might be right."

"It's not impossible," Robert said. "I'm afraid it's happened to me too."

"Oh no!" exclaimed Ellen as the others stared at him in alarm.

"I know from our previous adventure together that I can trust you ladies to be discreet, and I'm telling you about this only because I need your help. My cottage was ransacked sometime while I was gone, and I'm still trying to determine exactly what was taken. I was wondering if there might be a connection with this other robbery, but it doesn't sound like it."

"Wow," exclaimed Sandra. "That's pretty scary. I guess no one saw anything?"

"That's where I need your help," Robert replied. "I thought you all might be able to ask around discreetly and see if any stranger was seen on the campus and especially around the cottages a couple of weeks ago."

Before Harriet could speak about the light she may have seen in his cottage, Robert went on. "Unfortunately, there's more. One of the objects taken from my home was my gun. It was locked in its usual container in the closet, but someone found it and took it."

"That's very serious," said Laura. "If it were used in a crime, it could be traced back to you and cause you a lot of trouble."

"I'm afraid that's exactly what happened," Robert said.

"Oh no!" Ellen said.

Before he could continue, Emily appeared with their entrees.

"Is there anything else right now?" she asked after serving everyone.

"No, we're fine for now," replied Barbara. They all nodded; they were eager for Emily to leave so Robert could continue his story.

"So what did you find out?" Ellen asked, looking at Robert anxiously.

"The police told me that my gun had been found at a crime scene."

"What did you tell them?" Sandra asked worriedly.

"I told them I'd just returned from Florida and had reported the stolen gun to the State Department and FBI as soon as I found out it was missing. I told them to contact my FBI friend Steve. You remember him. He was the one who helped us when Laura was missing. Steve assured the police that because of my State Department association, the robbery had already been reported to the FBI. A few phone calls convinced them that I was indeed who I said I was. My story checked out. They haven't called me in again."

"What kind of crime was involved? Was it serious?" asked Laura.

"I'm afraid so," said Robert. "A man had been shot and killed in a hotel room in DC, and my gun was found nearby. Forensic tests indicated that it was the murder weapon, so naturally, I became a person of interest as they say."

The women stared in disbelief. Things like that happened only in mystery novels and movies. They had a sense of déjà vu as once again Robert was telling them about a real murder just as he had the previous year when Laura was missing. They could not believe this was happening again.

"Who was it? Someone you knew?" asked Barbara.

"He hasn't been positively identified yet. He'd been shot in the face and was unrecognizable. However, the hotel room was registered to an Alexei Solkov, a name I'm not familiar with."

Ellen shivered as she imagined the scene in the hotel room with a dead body that had been shot in the face lying in a pool of blood. This sounded like a murder mystery – not real life.

Harriet maintained her usual stoic calm and asking in a quiet voice, "What can we do? You indicated earlier that you wanted our help."

"I thought perhaps you could ask around to see whether any of the residents or staff had seen anything unusual or any strangers hanging about. Augusta was sent to clean the cottage the day before I returned and discovered the break-in. She immediately contacted Cathy Evans, who locked up the cottage until I could examine it. There were traces of footprints in the hall, probably where snow was tracked in."

Robert thought for a minute before continuing. "I spoke to John at the front desk, but no one had asked for me. Of course, anyone could look up my cottage number in the residents' directory, which can be found all over the campus."

No one had been eating while Robert was talking; they were engrossed in his story. But they finally turned to their meals as they thought about his story.

"I ordered the sea bass, and it's fine, but I miss Frank's delicious sauce," Karen said.

"That was smart," Barbara said. "This baked ham is okay too. The substitute chef is pretty good. It's just that we've gotten so used to Frank's magic touch."

"You're right," Laura added with a laugh. "I loaded up at the salad bar just in case the rest of the meal wasn't very good."

"I see what you mean," Robert said as he tasted the bass.

Harriet ignored her meal as she leaned toward Robert. "Robert, I may have seen something around your cottage, but I'm not sure. I thought at first that I saw a light in your cottage one night while you were gone, but in the morning, I decided it must have been the light from the streetlamp reflecting in your window. However, as you know, I saw the same light again a few days ago when you returned, and it made me think that perhaps I really did see something before."

Robert put down his fork and gave her his full attention. "The FBI were in the cottage taking photos and dusting for fingerprints last Wednesday night after I called them, so that's probably the light you saw then. But the earlier light may well have been the thief. Did you notice anything else? Anyone hanging around who didn't belong there?"

"Now that you mention it, there was a man in front of your cottage around that time. I was going to ask if I could help him find someone, but he scurried off before I had a chance to speak to him."

The rest of the table had paused in their meal to listen to Harriet.

Robert pressed her for more details. "Do you remember anything about him? Was he tall, short, lean, heavy? That sort of thing."

"I didn't get up close, and I probably wouldn't remember him at all except that it's so unusual to see a stranger here. Even most of the maintenance personnel are familiar to us, and we usually wave as they drive by in their golf carts going from building to building."

She paused wrinkling her forehead as she tried to recover the memory of the man she had seen in front of Robert's cottage. "He was a little shorter than me, so probably about five feet ten." She drew herself up straighter in her chair contemplating her own six-foot height. "He was rather slight. Dark hair. Fair complexion. Of course I couldn't see his eyes or any other facial features. Oh, but he did have a moustache. I remember because he reminded me of an old friend of my husband who had one."

"Harriet, your excellent memory certainly stands you in good stead here especially considering you saw him for such a brief time and at a distance. Your information should be very helpful for the police."

Harriet beamed at Robert's praise.

"You know, Robert, I think I may have seen him too," Barbara said hesitantly. "In fact, if it was the same man, I actually spoke to him."

"What do you remember about him?" Robert asked eagerly.

"I remember he had dark hair and a moustache. The moustache is what jogged my memory. He was wearing an overcoat, not a uniform like the maintenance men. He seemed to be middle aged, too young to be one of the residents, so I briefly wondered what he was doing here. At first, I assumed he was the son of a resident, but when I asked if he was looking for someone, he gave me a name I'd never heard of, so I suggested he go to the main desk in the lobby and they could help him."

"And did he?" asked Robert.

"No. He thanked me, and we exchanged a few pleasantries about the weather. He headed off away from the main building rather than toward it. I wondered about that too, but I decided it was none of my business. I thought perhaps he just wanted to look around before going to the main desk. I was in a hurry, so I didn't give it much thought."

"Do you remember what he said?" Robert asked.

"I don't remember the exact words, but he definitely had an accent – Eastern European maybe."

"Could it have been Russian?" asked Robert thinking about the missing file.

"Sure, it might have been Russian," Barbara replied thoughtfully.

"Can you describe his facial features in any more detail? I realize it was a couple of weeks ago, but you did see him up close," Robert said hopefully.

"I'm not sure I can describe him in words, but I could probably make a fairly accurate sketch. Perhaps

Harriet can help me since she saw him too even if at a distance. Between the two of us, we might be able to come up with something pretty close."

"Yes, I think I'd recognize him if I saw him again," Harriet said to Barbara. "So I might be able to give you some feedback as you work on a portrait."

"That's great!" Robert exclaimed.

"I'm too tired to begin it tonight, but we can start on it first thing in the morning if that's all right with you, Harriet," Barbara said.

Harriet nodded. "Sure, that's fine with me. I don't have anything planned that can't be rescheduled. I'll meet you in the art studio if that's where you want to work."

"No, I think the studio is too public. Why don't I bring my sketching materials to your cottage about eight thirty? I'm anxious to get going, and we'll have plenty of privacy there."

"Good. See you then," Harriet said.

Robert smiled broadly. "That's terrific. I hoped you all would be able to help in one way or another, but I didn't expect this much help."

He looked around at the six women, who were watching him intently. "One other thing. We're not telling anyone about the break-in. Cathy is concerned about scaring the other residents especially after the Cutler robbery. This would just raise everyone's anxiety even more, and it appears that this was not a random break-in but that I was targeted by someone who was interested in papers I had in my files. I'm not sure what he was after yet, but it may be related to the murder in the Washington hotel since my gun was involved. That would really freak out the residents, so please keep this between us."

The women nodded and murmured their assurances.

"I was sure I could count on the Tuesday Table Ladies to keep this quiet. We don't want to start a panic among the residents of Oakwood." Robert smiled warmly at his audience as they nodded. "Now, we better finish our dinner before it's even colder that it is already."

Barbara appeared at Harriet's cottage the next morning at 8:15 and said, "I hope I'm not too early. I was anxious to get started. I didn't even wait for my second cup of coffee."

"I can fix that. Cream or sugar?" Harriet asked as she poured coffee into a mug.

"No, just black please. Can we sit here at the dining table to work on the sketch?"

"Yes. I see you brought your sketchbook and pencils. I hope we can come up with something that will be helpful to Robert and the police," Harriet said as she took a chair next to Barbara.

"As I recall, his face was oval-shaped, like this, and his cheeks were somewhat sunken." Barbara began to draw as she talked making a series of firm marks on the sketch paper and shading the cheeks until she was satisfied with the effect.

"Yes, and he had heavy, dark eyebrows," Harriet added. "Yes, just like that. I wasn't close enough to see his eyes."

"His eyes were small and close together. They were muddy brown, like coffee with a little milk stirred in," Barbara noted. "I noticed because they were like my grandfather's eyes."

"The most memorable part was the moustache. It seemed European for some reason. It curled up at the ends like that Agatha Christie character – what's his name?" Harriet asked.

"You're right. Hercule Poirot is usually portrayed with a moustache like that. I knew he reminded me of someone." Barbara added a Poirot-type moustache to her portrait and began to fill in the dark hair.

"What about his mouth?" asked Harriet. "I couldn't see it very well."

Barbara closed her eyes for a moment as she tried to visualize the man she had spoken to. "His lips were straight and almost colorless," she said thoughtfully. "They were hard to see clearly under the moustache, but I think they were something like this." She began to outline the lips with almost no shading.

The two women spent the morning bent over the sketch. Barbara erased a line here and adding a few lines there, darkening one area while making another a little lighter as she responded to Harriet's feedback.

Finally, Harriet said, "I think you got him," as she rose and took a few steps back to view the portrait from a distance.

Barbara propped up the drawing and stepped across the room to view it. "Yes, it certainly looks a lot like the man I spoke to, and I gather he's the man you saw too. He had a scarf around his neck, so I didn't get a good look at that. I'll do what I can."

She sat and quickly sketched in a scarf and a small patch of the coat she remembered. She didn't think the police would want a full-length sketch – they would be interested mostly in the face.

"That's the best I can do without seeing him again," Barbara said as she stepped back again and studied her handiwork.

"I think it's great. I envy your talent," Harriet said. "That certainty looks like the man I saw."

"I have to run now. Can you get it to Robert?" asked Barbara as she put on her jacket.

"Sure. I'll get an envelope and leave it at Robert's door if he's not home."

"We did what we could. I hope it helps. I'd hate to see him in any trouble," Barbara said as she went out the door.

CHAPTER TWELVE

A Night Out

Friendship is when people know all about you but like you anyway.

—ANONYMOUS

The next morning, Robert mulled over Harriet's and Barbara's revelations at the dinner meeting. He thought it unlikely that the Tuesday Table Ladies would be able to shed any light on the identity of the mysterious intruder. However, having observed them in action at the time of Laura's disappearance, he thought it just might be worthwhile to inform them about the robbery. It was at best a long shot, but they were generally observant and shrewd, and he welcomed the thought that they might possibly have noticed something. He felt sure he could depend on them to keep what he told them confidential.

It was likely that any would-be thief would have made himself familiar with the layout of the campus before trying anything. Strangers were always objects of curiosity especially as there would be fewer of them in the winter. During his years abroad, he had learned the value of taking notice of anything unusual even if it seemed insignificant. Harriet, who had a practiced and critical eye, was always observant of people. Barbara had the discernment of an artist. He was not surprised they had taken note of the stranger. It depended on their memory and ability to capture in the drawing what they had seen.

He needed to bring Cathy up to date, but he decided to wait until Barbara and Harriet produced the sketch so he could show it to her. If it was anything like the man, she might be able to account for his presence at Oakwood. No need to interrupt her day, he thought. He would ask her to have dinner at their favorite off-campus restaurant. He wanted to do that anyway, and this was a good excuse for doing so. As the past gradually receded into memory, he was increasingly aware of how much she meant to him. Dinner with her was always enjoyable.

Having confirmed the arrangements with Cathy, he made the table reservation. *I wonder if she enjoys our dinners as much as I do?* He found himself uncharacteristically uncertain. He had always taken her for granted. She had become his friend only because of Gary, and Gary was gone.

He spent that afternoon tending to his car. He had not driven it since his return, and it would not start when he tried it; he had been away too long. Fortunately, AAA came to his rescue promptly; the driver was delighted to see to a vintage Jaguar. As soon as the mechanic got the engine purring again, Robert drove to the nearest car wash. The result was a lustrous racing-green ride ready to pick up Cathy for their evening out. His self-assurance returned.

On his return to his cottage, he found a large envelope at his front door. It was from Harriet, and it held the sketch she and Barbara had offered to develop. A note enclosed said that they each agreed it was a pretty good likeness. He was glad of its arrival just in time to show Cathy at dinner. Unless she could confidently account for his presence at Oakwood, he would take it to the authorities the next day. Maybe the Tuesday Table Ladies had come to *his* rescue this time.

Cathy was ready when he arrived. She was wearing a close-fitting and beautifully tailored but simple dress of a lustrous, deep turquoise. She was tall and slender, and she looked elegant. He was used to seeing her in her workaday clothes. His actress mother would have called them sensible when in her prima donna mood, but this was not sensible. He reluctantly helped her on with her coat. Too bad one needed to bundle up in the cold weather, he thought.

She carefully locked the door and turned around to admire Robert's chariot, which reflected the thorough cleaning it had endured that afternoon.

As he helped her negotiate the Jaguar's low seating, he paid her the usual compliment. "You're looking elegant, Cathy." It was his routine compliment, but that time, he really meant it. She rewarded him with a warm smile and settled in the passenger seat.

"I've been looking forward to this evening," He said. Another ordinary remark but that time truly felt.

They drove in thoughtful silence to their favorite restaurant, which was some distance from Oakwood. Each sensed that something was different, but neither could find words to explain it. The mood changed as they drove up to the entrance. The owner came out and greeted them effusively. He offered to park the car for Robert. He had been eagerly waiting his chance to drive the Jaguar. Cathy looked curiously at the envelope Robert picked up from the back seat as they got out of the car, but she said nothing.

Their table was by a large window overlooking a manicured lawn. In the last phases of winter, it might have looked rather desolate but for a resilient array of evergreens. The room was warm and welcoming. Robert seated Cathy and sat down across from her. At their places were handwritten menus detailing the choices for the day. There were never more than a few, but they were always freshly prepared. They made their selections, and Robert ordered a carafe of the house wine, which was always reliable.

"It's so good to be here. I do look forward to our dinners. It's a world away from Oakwood. Much as I enjoy my work, it feels good to get away." Cathy relaxed with a happy sigh.

"I'm sorry, Cathy, but I have to bring you back to Oakwood. Before we settle down, I feel I should tell you what's happened. Then we can enjoy our evening."

Cathy was puzzled and even anxious, but she nodded indicating he should continue.

"As you know, I reported the loss of the Russian file and my gun to Washington. Since then, I received a call from the local police asking me to come to their office to answer some questions. I went there right away and learned that my gun had been found in the hotel room of a man who had been shot to death. An alarming, uncomfortable, and prolonged interview followed. The first question was why I hadn't reported the theft to them. I explained the protocol that I had followed, but it must have sounded like a poor excuse to them, and I wondered whether they believed me. I gave them contact information to verify my story. They also asked my whereabouts at a time when I was in Florida and people who could account for my presence there.

"I was rather shaken at this experience. I've never been a suspect in a police investigation before. I've dealt with many government officials in my career, but I've never been interrogated like that in a police station. Once, I had to bail out a young US citizen in another country who'd run afoul of the local law, but I've never been subject to it myself. It was very humiliating." He sounded deeply upset as he recalled the experience.

"Oh, Robert, how awful! What did you do?" Cathy was shocked.

"At the first opportunity, I reached out to my FBI friend, Steve, who could verify at least some of my story. He quickly came to my rescue. He assured them that because of my previous associations, the robbery had already been reported to the FBI. A few phone calls convinced them that I was who I said I was, and Steve was able to escort me out of there. I hope that is the end of the story, but it probably isn't. The man was murdered, and it was my gun that killed him."

Cathy was speechless, but thoughts raced through her mind. *How could this have happened to Robert of all people? Is something in his past catching up with him? Or is this all a terrible mistake?*

"I thought about it a lot when I got home as you can imagine. Perhaps the clue is in the identity and motive of whoever broke into my cottage. He took my gun. It seemed to me that someone planning to break into a residence at Oakwood would have found his way onto the campus to get a good feel for the layout. He might have gotten hold of a map, but there's nothing like actually experiencing a place if you're assessing potential access or escape routes." He paused and saw that Cathy was listening intently.

"Now, especially in the colder months, anyone not a resident might have been noticed by someone here even if he had been posing as a technician or a repair man. I assume it was a man." Encouraged by a nod from Cathy, he went on. "So I took a chance when I had dinner last evening with the Tuesday Table Ladies."

He paused. Cathy, realizing what he was about to say, looked worried. He took a deep breath and went on. He wanted her to know. "I told them about the break-in and my missing file. I asked them to think back a few weeks to see whether they might have seen something or someone unusual. Harriet doesn't miss much. She told me she'd noticed a man she couldn't identify. So did Barbara, who paints portraits and looks for interesting subjects. They worked together today to see if they could sketch what they remembered of the stranger. Who knows, Cathy? They might have something."

Despite his optimistic tone, Cathy continued to look anxious.

He hastily continued. "The Tuesday Table Ladies all agreed to keep all this confidential. I stressed how important it was not to start a rumor that could upset the other residents. I'm sure they understood. But I worry that you may think it was a risk I shouldn't have taken. The last thing I want is to worry you and spoil this lovely evening."

Cathy received all this in silence. It was disconcerting. The last thing she wanted was word of a break-in circulating around Oakwood. She could not deny that it had happened, but she was not at liberty to have announced the event herself and reassure the residents that because of the circumstances, there was nothing for them to be concerned about.

Robert waited uneasily. He knew how important the well-being of Oakwood was to her. It was her life. He also faced the growing realization of how important she was to him. He wanted to tell her the whole story.

"I have the sketch the Tuesday Table Ladies produced, and I'd be grateful if you'd take a look at it. Let me know if you recognize him. Of course, it's drawn from memory and only an approximation at best."

He opened the envelope, handed her the drawing, and waited. She took her time looking at it. She shook her head. "I'm sorry, Robert, but he's a total stranger to me." She lapsed into silence. She needed time to absorb what she had heard. It was so unexpected and unsettling.

She looked at Robert, whose face was a picture of apprehension. She said, "If I didn't know something about your history, I might have been very annoyed that you didn't alert me sooner about all this. As it is, I confess to being concerned. You did take a chance, but I too think it's possible the Tuesday Table Ladies can keep quiet about this. I for one would be greatly relieved to see the culprit apprehended."

She knew that as a resident of Oakwood living independently, he was free to follow his intuition, but on the other hand, as a member of the community, he was to use that responsibility wisely. Perhaps this would work out for the best for everyone. There wasn't anything she could do about it at that point. Besides, he had clearly been unnerved by his experience with the police, who seemed to be looking at him as a possible suspect.

The wine arrived. Cathy smiled. "I could do with a drink, Robert."

Feeling he had been at least partially reprieved, he smiled ruefully and filled their wine glasses. He wanted to propose a toast but found himself uncertain of what to say.

"Here's to us, Cathy," he offered tentatively.

She looked up at him and slowly raised her glass. "To you, Robert."

CHAPTER THIRTEEN
New Information

A work of art is the evidence offered by a
fantastically observant witness.

—JOHN BANVILLE

Robert awoke with a smile the next morning thinking of the previous evening and the delightful dinner with Cathy. After his rather sheepish confession and her reluctant acceptance of his explanation, the evening had gone very well. She was so easy to talk to. He realized he had communicated more than he had intended, but he didn't regret that. He wondered when it might be appropriate to ask her for dinner again.

After his shower, he dressed slowly giving more attention than usual to his attire before preparing his coffee and cranberry-orange scone. He retrieved the *Washington Post* from his doorstep and settled in a comfortable easy chair to enjoy his breakfast. He was still under the spell of the previous evening.

The peaceful tableau was suddenly shattered by the demanding ring of the telephone. It was Steve.

"How's it going, Rob?" he asked soberly.

"I assume you're asking if I've found anything important missing from my files," Robert replied. "A lot of my notes on Russia are gone, but I can't think of anything that was highly secret. They were more in the way of personal notes about my experiences – people I met and places I traveled to. I met many interesting characters in my six years in Moscow, and I wanted to include them in my memoirs. I'm afraid I'm going to have a hard time reconstructing some of those notes. It'll make writing my book a lot harder. So far, nothing helpful, but I do have something else for you. I was going to call you today. I have something to show you that might be very useful."

"We can use all the help you can give us, but I have some information for you too. I'd rather not talk over the phone. Can we meet for lunch?"

"Sure. How about at one at the Chesapeake Grill, where we met last time when we visited Eduardo in the hospital?"

"Sounds good. See you then."

Robert hung up slowly and wondered what had spooked Steve so much. *He seemed anxious to get off the phone. Or was that just the natural caution of an experienced FBI agent? I'll find out soon enough.*

He finished the newspaper and wrote a couple of thank-you notes to his Florida friends before starting out for the restaurant. He hoped Steve had some good news for him concerning the DC shooting victim.

He spotted Steve's old black government Ford as he pulled into the restaurant parking lot. The racing-green Jaguar stood out among the more modest cars surrounding it, and Robert smiled as he stopped to wipe a smudge off the hood. His mother would have been pleased that he had kept her car in such good condition.

He joined Steve at a corner booth and asked anxiously, "What have you found out about the murder?" as he placed the envelope with Barbara's sketch on the table.

"Well Rob, they've identified the guy who was killed with your gun. He was a wealthy Russian who was over here to explore some real estate investments. He was going by the name of Alexei Solkov according to the hotel register," Steve said quietly.

"I still don't recognize the name," said Robert slowly.

"They think that may not be his real name," Steve replied. "They're still checking. It's possible that if he was already known to the authorities, he may have adopted a new identity to get into the country."

"Do they know why he was murdered?" Robert asked.

"No, and they don't have any suspects except you of course. Unfortunately, something else turned up in his room that ties you to the murder. They found a notebook written in Russian, and your name was mentioned several times. They've turned it over to a translator and should have some answers soon. In the meantime, that ties him directly to you, so you're at the top of their list of suspects. Also, the gun was wiped clean, so there's no chance of identifying the killer through prints on the gun. Sorry to bring you such bad news, but I'm sure it will be straightened out soon. In the meantime, you can expect another call from the police for further interrogation. They may pull you into the station again. They're checking out your contacts in Florida."

"Oh great!" Robert sighed. The euphoria from the previous evening was gone. "Do they have anything else?"

"They don't think it was a robbery since his wallet was in his pocket and his belongings seemed to be intact. And he was wearing some expensive rings that hadn't been touched. It doesn't look like a common robbery. He'd been in Washington about a month and had been seen all over town schmoozing with the local businessmen and trying to make a deal for some upscale condos and hotels in Washington. He'd even been to a Foreign Service party, but they aren't sure who had brought him there. They're trying to track that down."

They were interrupted by the waiter, who took their orders – a cheeseburger and fries for Steve and crab cakes for Robert – his favorite – and draft beers for both.

"The Foreign Service connection is interesting – another reason for the police to be interested in me. They should be able to follow up on that pretty quickly. If they can find who invited him, it would be helpful," Robert said thoughtfully. "That might be the tie-in to the theft in my cottage. I can't relax until I know what they were looking for in my cottage and how my gun ended up involved in a murder. I keep wondering if someone was trying to set me up."

"That's certainly a possibility. Let's hope they sort it out real soon. You said you had some info for me."

Robert waited until the server had set down their beers before pulling the sketch out. "You remember my telling you about the Tuesday Table Ladies when you were involved in Eduardo's murder. I thought I could count on their discretion, so I told them about the theft in my cottage and asked if they'd seen anyone hanging around my cottage or anything unusual around the time of the break-in. We don't get many strangers hanging around in the winter. Fortunately, a couple of them had seen someone. Harriet lives in the cottage next to mine, and she had noticed someone in front of my cottage while I was away. Barbara had actually spoken to the man, and she said he had an accent that might have been Eastern European or even Russian."

Steve studied the sketch carefully. "This is quite good. One of the women did this?"

"Yes. Barbara's an artist as well as a lawyer, and she and Harriet, who is an astute observer, worked together to come up with this image of the stranger they'd seen. I don't recognize him, but it might be helpful to the police, and the FBI might have something on him especially if he's Russian."

They were interrupted again by the arrival of their food. They paused long enough to take a few bites.

"This could be very useful," Steve said. "I'll send a copy to the FBI facial recognition software team and circulate it among the DC FBI agents and the police. Hopefully, someone will come up with an ID. This may be the break we've been looking for." He carefully placed the sketch in its envelope and turned back to his lunch.

"I have another question, Steve. Why were you so hush-hush over the phone? It seemed you didn't want to say anything until we met in person."

"You're right, Rob. It's this Russian connection. They have people all over the DC area, and everything's bugged. I know our guys checked your place for bugs, but the technology improves so fast that it's all we can do to keep up with it. So we're trying to be extra careful with this case at least until we know who and what we're dealing with."

"I wish I could figure out what in my Russian notes might be relevant to this murder. There must be some connection I haven't found yet."

"Let me know if you find anything," Steve said. "I think the solution may lie with the identity of the victim. Is he really Alexei Solkov, or is he hiding another identity behind that name?"

"Changing the subject, how are things going with you and Lindsey? We didn't have a chance to talk when you rescued me from that police station. I'm afraid my mind was on other things."

Robert and Steve had met on a case for the State Department some years before, and though Steve was considerably younger, they had become good friends and tried to stay in touch; they met occasionally for lunch or dinner. He had met Steve's live-in girlfriend, Lindsey, several times and was fond of her too.

Steve replied with a grin. "Believe it or not, after all these years, we've decided to take the plunge and make it legal. We're getting married next month, and I want you to come to the wedding."

"Wow! That's a surprise. So she's willing to put up with you for the long haul? You're a lucky guy."

"Yeah, I know it. I decided I'd better make sure she didn't give up on me. Besides, she wants to have a couple of kids, so we can't wait much longer. Can you imagine me as a father?"

"You'll be a great father! But I hope the kids have Lindsey's looks," Robert said laughing. "Give her my best. She's a wonderful girl."

After paying their separate checks, the two walked to the parking lot.

"Thanks for the sketch. I think it'll help. I'll pass on a copy to the police right away so they'll have it before they interrogate you again. Hopefully, I'll have some good news before too long."

"I'll let you know if any other notes are missing from my files. I'm going through them again to see if I overlooked anything the first time," Robert said as he climbed into the Jag. He backed out of the parking spot with extra care and headed home.

He thought about Steve's surprising announcement as he drove back to Oakwood. He tried imagining how Steve's life might change after the wedding. Probably quite a bit if they decided to have children. He wondered, as he sometimes did, what kind of a father he himself might have been but decided that point was moot. But if things had worked out differently in Italy all those years ago, he might have found out. Any sons he would have had would have been middle aged now – a sobering thought. He considered all he had missed without a wife and family.

He shook his head to clear his thoughts. Instead of thinking about what might have been, he had better prepare himself for another encounter with the police. He didn't have anything to add to his previous statement, but they would undoubtedly press him for further details. He would get back to the files as soon as he got home and try again to find some clue to what the thief had been searching for.

CHAPTER FOURTEEN
Aspiring Writers

*There really must be a corpse in a detective novel
and the deader the corpse the better.*
— S. S. VAN DYNE

While Robert and Steve were having lunch, the Tuesday Table Ladies were gathering for a meeting to discuss the proposed scenarios for their mystery novel. They had agreed to meet at Harriet's cottage with their notes from the previous meetings. Harriet collected coats and jackets and put them on a bed in the guest room while Ellen and Karen sat on two comfortable easy chairs in the living room. Laura and Barbara arrived together happy to move into the warmth of the cottage after walking across the Oakwood campus on the brisk, late-March afternoon. Sandra put her laptop on a table in the living room.

"I thought this would be easier than moving your desktop into the living room," she told Harriet.

Harriet's computer was set up in the bedroom, which was too small to fit all six women comfortably. "It'll take just a minute to connect with the internet if you can give me your network name and password."

Harriet handed her a card with the information, and Sandra sighed with relief when the familiar icon signaling an internet connection appeared. "Okay, we're all set here," she said cheerily.

Harriet indicated the pitchers of iced tea and water on the dining room table as well as a pot of freshly made coffee along with sugar and cream. "Help yourselves. I don't have any cookies, but I figured we'd all just eaten lunch. If you didn't, let me know and I can fix you something."

They all assured her that they didn't need any food; they happily poured themselves drinks.

"I have some news," Sandra announced. "Elizabeth Cutler's jewelry has been found. Finally!"

"Where was it then?" Ellen asked eagerly. They all wanted to know.

"It turns out that in all the excitement, Elizabeth had not considered that the Sunday visit from her four-year-old granddaughter Susan might be relevant. Elizabeth had forgotten that while she was on a lengthy phone call in the living room, Susan was playing in the bedroom. Apparently, she'd picked up the jewelry from the dresser and after trying it on, she wanted to put it where she could find it next time she came to visit. In any case, Nora found it in a large vase sitting on the floor in the corner. When Nora picked up the vase to vacuum under it, she heard the jewelry rattling about inside. Elizabeth asked Susan about it and finally solved the mystery."

"I'm sure Susan would have found the jewelry irresistible. I remember playing with my grandmother's jewelry when I was little. It would put on her necklaces and admire myself in the mirror," Ellen said.

"I knew it!" said Harriet. "I hope she's apologized properly to Augusta."

"That'll never happen. She's much too stubborn to admit how wrong she was," Barbara said.

"I'm afraid you're right," Harriet replied.

Sandra's face showed her disgust. "All that fuss for nothing. And the way she blamed other people ..."

"Poor Augusta. To be put through all that for no reason," Barbara said bitterly.

"Yes, some people actually changed housekeepers because of Elizabeth's accusations. I expect there'll be a few who will always be suspicious of Augusta," Ellen suggested.

"You're right!" Sandra agreed.

"I'm glad she found it and her suspicions will be put to rest for most of the residents," Laura said. "Now, we'd better get to work if we want to get anything done. Fortunately, Robert didn't ask about the book at dinner. It will be fun to surprise him when we have a chapter or two on paper. So where should we start?"

"Why don't you read us what you have on Harriet's scenario, and then we'll read the online dating proposal. We can see where to go from there." Sandra seated herself next to the laptop.

"Would you summarize it for us, Laura? I think you took the most notes," Harriet suggested.

"Okay, but you two chime in if I leave something out," Laura agreed. "Can you all hear me all right?"

"Yes, that's fine," said Harriet, who had the most severe hearing impairment among the group.

"Our story takes place in a retirement community similar to Oakwood, but we've set it in Florida instead of Maryland. We haven't yet named our leading character, a female resident of the community, because we want to make sure we don't choose a name of anyone here. Every time someone suggested a name, someone else would point out a resident with the same first name. We may end up with a name like Victoria or Desdemona to avoid a conflict."

"How about Ophelia?" asked Ellen eliciting a burst of laughter from the group.

"The heroine is a retired school teacher in her midseventies who was widowed several years earlier. She's chair of an education committee not unlike our

Harriet," she said smiling at Harriet. "When the story begins, she's expecting a prominent author to speak that evening. The event has been in the planning for months, and our unnamed heroine is very excited at the prospect of meeting her distinguished guest. She's carefully prepared her opening remarks and has asked the local paper to cover the event, which is expected to be much bigger than the usual monthly presentation. Several outsiders have expressed an interest in attending. She was fortunate in scheduling the author because he was planning to visit a sister who lived nearby and who had mentioned the visit to a friend at the retirement community. We haven't named that yet either."

"That's even harder than naming the characters," Barbara interjected. "We don't want to be sued."

"When he fails to appear at the agreed-upon time, she gets very worried about informing the audience that the speaker is a no-show. At first, she is convinced that he's caught in traffic or lost on the unfamiliar highways. Since he has her cell phone number, she's sure he'll contact her before the lecture is to begin, but she hears nothing and is forced to apologize to the audience and send them on their way. The heroine calls his sister, but she hasn't heard from him either. He was planning to come to her home after the lecture. Our heroine decides to wait in the lobby, hoping to hear from the speaker and thinking that if he lost her phone number, he would surely contact the retirement community." Laura stopped for a sip of tea.

"Has this ever happened to you, Harriet?" asked Ellen while Laura took a quick break.

"No, but I've had a couple who walked in just when the lecture was to start or even a few minutes late."

"Anyway, after an hour or so, the security guard rushes into the lobby to call the police to report a dead body he found in a car outside the building. Of course, it's our speaker, and the heroine must inform the sister of her brother's death. She feels responsible for bringing him onto the campus and regrets that she didn't pick him up at the airport instead of letting him rent a car to drive to the retirement community. She and her friends begin to investigate the victim's background to see why he might have been murdered. They're convinced it wasn't a random hit but a planned murder.

"The police detective assigned to the case – also yet unnamed – is the son of an old friend, and our heroine works with him to solve the crime. It turns out that the victim had been killed by a gang that he had contacted to use as models for the characters in his next novel. The gang leader was afraid too many of their activities would be revealed, and he was not sure he could trust the author to maintain the confidentiality of his sources. He suspected that the author might actually be working undercover for the police. There are a couple of subplots with some of the other characters, but that gives you a rough outline of what we have in mind."

She looked at Harriet and Barbara. "Do you two want to add anything?"

"Not I. You've summed it up very nicely," Barbara replied.

Harriet shook her head. The others asked a few questions, and there was some discussion about the other possible characters.

"I like the idea of using a retirement community as a setting," Karen said. "We certainly know enough to write about one. We could include all sorts of details that would make it more real."

"We want to hear what you all have come up with," said Barbara. "Who's going to report on your story?"

"I will," replied Sandra. "It's something I started, so I guess I need to follow up. As you know, we have a main character who is interested in exploring online dating. Samantha had a bad experience with her last boyfriend, so she decides to try online dating because she thinks the guys will have been thoroughly screened before they were listed on the site. Unfortunately, she's mistaken in that, and she gets herself in even worse trouble than with her previous boyfriends."

"How old is she?" asked Laura. "And what does she do for a living?"

"We haven't decided whether she's retirement age or much younger – in her midthirties for example. And of course that affects whether she's working. Ellen would like her to be younger to make the book sexier. Karen and I think we might do better with an older character, closer to our own ages especially since this is our first novel." She looked around the room. "What do you guys think?"

"I think it depends on the plot. Why don't you tell us more about it?" Laura suggested.

"Briefly, Samantha finally finds someone she thinks she'd like to meet and has several dates with him. She's intrigued by his French accent and his European style. She's really attracted to him, and she's beginning to think this might be a serious relationship when they happen to run into some of his friends who ask about his wife. Samantha becomes enraged, and as soon as the friends leave, she attacks him verbally. They have a big fight. She calls a taxi and goes home. He calls her repeatedly the next day until she finally agrees to listen to his explanation. He insists that he and his wife were about to separate and that he cares deeply for Samantha. She agrees to meet him in the park, but when she arrives at the spot they've chosen, she finds his body. He'd been stabbed, and the knife is lying nearby. Of course she's accused of the murder, so she and her friends set out to find the real killer and clear her name.

"Obviously, who her friends are depends on whether she's thirty or seventy. We keep coming back to that basic question – it affects the plot in so many ways," Ellen said.

"In any case, they eventually find out that the wife is the killer and Samantha is exonerated," Sandra said. "As you can see, there are still lots of details to be worked out if we decide to go with this scenario. I have to admit that we spent most of the meeting online exploring various sites to get a better idea of how finding a date online works."

"It was very interesting," Karen said. "You get so much information. It's a little overwhelming. All those people out there looking …"

A lively discussion ensued as the women explored the possibilities of the two plots.

"We could all have a lot of fun on the dating sites as we research them for the story," Ellen said.

"But we could do that without writing a novel about it," Barbara replied. "It sounds like a pretty complicated plot for a first novel."

"We certainly know enough about retirement communities to write a believable novel about one," Karen suggested.

"But that's so boring compared to online dating," Ellen protested. "And I still think we need to make it sexy or else no one will want to buy it."

"We could introduce lots of interesting characters in a retirement community. We certainly know enough of them here," Harriet said.

"If we disguise them so we aren't sued …" Barbara said.

After considerable back and forth about the two scenarios, Laura suggested they were not ready to decide and should think about it for a few days. "After all, if we decide to do this, it'll take months or even years to write, so we all need to agree before we start. I think each of us should play around with these ideas during the week and make our decision at dinner next Tuesday."

Everyone agreed to that; they were relieved that at least something had been decided even if it was just to postpone the decision.

CHAPTER FIFTEEN

Answers

Cinema can fill the empty spaces of life and loneliness.

—PEDRO ALMODOVAR

A few afternoons later, Robert answered a knock on the door and found Steve on his doorstep. "This is a surprise. Come on in," said Robert as he stepped aside and Steve entered.

"I have some good news, and I thought you'd like to hear about it in person," Steve said as he removed his windbreaker. "I was nearby, and my cell's on the fritz. I thought I'd take a chance and just drop by. I hope it's okay."

"I'm delighted to see you especially if you have some good news. Can I fix you a drink?"

"Sure. Scotch and soda if you have it," said Steve as he followed Robert into the kitchen.

Drinks in hand, the two men settled into a couple of easy chairs in the living room. Steve pulled a paper from his pocket.

"Well, first, they have the killer in custody. He's being arraigned tomorrow. With the sketch you provided, our FBI colleagues were able to identify him very quickly. It took some doing to locate him, but when they did, he didn't put up any resistance, and he's now dealing with the DC police from a cell. They have a couple of witnesses who've placed him in the hotel on the day of the shooting, and they're running his prints against some they found in the hotel room."

With an obvious sense of relief, Robert said, "That's great! Who is this guy, and why did he kill this Alexei if that's his name?"

"The killer's name is Leo Petrov. Apparently, he's a minor player in the local Russian mafia – mostly involved in intimidation and extortion of Russian immigrants with shady backgrounds. He threatens to report them to the police unless they pay up. But occasionally, he does a job for some of the bigwigs, and that's what happened here."

"So who was he working for when he vandalized my cottage?"

"That's the interesting part. He was working for the guy he killed. Alexei's real name was Ivan Fedorov. Do you recognize it?"

"I sure do!" Robert exclaimed. "I had a couple of run-ins with him when I was attached to the Moscow embassy. He was KGB and apparently assigned to keep an eye on me, which he did with great enthusiasm. Every time I turned around, there he was watching me. It seemed like he wanted me to know he was there as a kind of subtle or not-so-subtle intimidation. It was most annoying, but after a while, I got used to it."

"Apparently, he'd moved way up in the Russian hierarchy in recent years," Steve said. "He'd made a fortune in real estate and came to the US to do some deals. He had close ties to the Putin government, so there's no telling what he was really after, but he clearly saw you as a threat to his cover. We suspect he was still working with Russian intelligence and perhaps was involved in a blackmail scheme or money laundering. Our killer, who is singing like a bird, tells us that Ivan had heard that you were writing a book about your experiences in Russia and was afraid you might talk about him. He'd overheard your name mentioned at the Foreign Service party he attended and asked about your whereabouts. Someone mentioned you had retired and were living here, so he hired Leo to see if you had any papers that could implicate him. He didn't want to be outed as KGB or the modern equivalent, and he wanted to make sure you didn't have anything that could identify him and interfere with his assignment whatever that was. You're lucky he didn't ask Leo to just get rid of you altogether. If he had, Ivan would still be alive."

Robert paled at the implication.

"But Leo had carried out his job. Why would he kill the guy who hired him?" Robert asked.

"Seems that when he reported to Ivan, they argued because Leo didn't bring the file he'd taken. He'd decided it was worth a lot more than Ivan was paying him, and he demanded more money. Ivan was incensed that Leo would try to hold him up like that. He didn't believe Leo had even been in your cottage, and he refused to pay him anything unless Leo turned over the file."

"That sounds like Ivan," Robert said. "Always suspicious of everyone and everything. Very useful for a KGB operative but not so much in other realms."

"Leo was insulted that Ivan didn't believe him. He grew more and more angry, and the two exchanged words. When Ivan threatened to report him to his Mafia bosses, Leo became enraged and pulled out your gun to threaten him. Ivan grabbed for the gun, which went off. Ivan was killed with the first bullet. Leo claims it was an accident. Says he didn't mean to shoot. Since it was your gun, he decided to leave it there rather than chance getting caught with it, and he thought it might even implicate you – which of course it did."

"This really is good news," said Robert with relief. "I think I'll have another drink to celebrate. How about you?"

"I better not. I have to drive back. But actually, Lindsay's is out with her women's group tonight, so I'm not in any hurry to get home."

"Great! Why don't you stay for dinner? It's Tuesday night, so I can introduce you to the Tuesday Table Ladies in the dining room."

"Good, I want to thank them for their help. Without that sketch, the police would still be looking for the killer and you'd still be their principal suspect." Steve held out his empty glass. "In that case, I'll join you in a celebratory drink."

Sandra was already seated at the table when Harriet arrived at the dining room that evening.

"Guess what?" Sandra exclaimed as Harriet sat in her usual chair. "Frank's back! I'm looking forward to tonight's dinner."

"That's good. We certainly have missed his deft touch in the kitchen. The meals haven't been bad, but not up to Frank's usual standard."

The two were soon joined by the others, who were equally happy to hear of Frank's return.

"Before we start, does anyone want to see the movie in the ballroom tonight?" Sandra asked eagerly, hoping to find someone to go with her. But they had all seen *Chariots of Fire* and didn't want to see it again even though it was highly rated.

"I'm watching that series on the queen on PBS tonight," said Barbara. "I don't want to miss it." The others nodded.

Emily appeared with menus as the women were discussing Frank's return, but she couldn't tell them anything about the conference he had attended.

"I really don't know anything. It's been so busy since he got back this evening, and I haven't spoken with him. Tonight's special is duck breast with a cherry glaze." She quickly took their orders and returned with waters and wine glasses.

"I have a bit of interesting news," Barbara announced. "They've identified the group behind the internet scam that's been in all the news lately. Apparently, the scam was being carried out by some teenagers in India. It's amazing how some young people have mastered the intricacies of the internet so early. I'm still struggling with Facebook and Instagram."

"Me too," added Laura. "Unless you use it all the time, it's hard to keep up with all the changes."

"You're right," Harriet said. "It changes so quickly. There seems to be a new update every day. I just can't keep up. Fortunately, we're bringing in a speaker to talk about email, Instagram, and Facebook. I think we could all use a review even if we're already using social media. It may encourage those who aren't to try out some new platforms."

"It certainly helps us to stay in touch with our children and especially our grandchildren," Sandra added.

"Did anyone notice that the forsythia bushes on the side of Riverview are blooming?" Barbara asked happily.

"Yes, and the leaves are out on the oak trees along the driveway," Laura said. "I think spring's finally on its way."

"I even saw a couple of sailboats on the river this afternoon," Harriet said with a smile. "And the robins have been in my bird feeder this week. It seems we've survived another winter on the Chesapeake."

"I think that deserves a toast," said Sandra laughing. "Here's to spring," she said holding up her wine glass as the others happily joined in.

Emily returned with soups and salads, and Ellen and Laura made their way to the salad bar. When everyone was seated again, Sandra announced, "We need to make some decisions about our mystery novel. First, do we want to try our hand at it? If so, which scenario should we pursue?" She looked around the table of potential authors.

"I think we should give it a go," said Ellen. "What do we have to lose?"

"Nothing," Barbara said. "Although as we get older, time increases in value. I could be drawing or painting with those hours. I'm sure we all have projects we may have to postpone for a while if we start this project, but I'm eager to see if we can do it."

Even Harriet agreed that it might be fun to try writing a mystery novel, so the next question was the scenario. Before they could begin discussing that, Emily appeared with the entrees – duck breast for Sandra, Laura, and Harriet, stir-fried chicken for Karen, and sesame crusted cod for Ellen and Barbara.

"I can tell Frank is back," said Karen as she tasted her meal. "This sauce on the chicken is delicious. It definitely has Frank's special touch."

"So does the cod," Ellen said. "It's great to have him back wherever he was."

"Oh look. There's Robert, and he seems to be headed for our table." Sandra nodded in Robert's direction as he and Steve approached the Tuesday Table.

"Good evening, ladies. I don't want to interrupt your dinner, but I have someone who'd like to meet you. This is my friend Steve, whom you've heard me talk about."

The women looked up with broad smiles. Laura said, "We're delighted to finally meet you, Steve. You were such a big help in dealing with Eduardo. I really appreciate what you did."

"This is the missing Laura Lambert, whom you helped us find," Robert told Steve. He introduced each of the women and paused to point out Barbara as the sketch artist with Harriet's help.

"Thanks to you two, the murderer has been caught and jailed. The sketch you provided was all the FBI needed to get an identification, and the police were able to track him down. He's confessed to the burglary and the shooting, so Robert here's officially off the hook."

Murmurs of relief were expressed around the table, and the two men chatted briefly with the Tuesday Table Ladies.

"The other good news is that the police have recovered my stolen file, and though they'll need it for the trial, they've agreed to make copies of the contents for me to use in the meantime so I'll be able to work on my book. We won't interrupt your dinner any longer. Our table is waiting by the window," Robert said.

"In case you haven't heard, Frank is back, and every dish is excellent tonight," Sandra said. "We can definitely tell the difference."

"I'm glad to hear that. You came for dinner on the right night," Robert said to Steve. "I'll explain over dinner." The men strolled to their table.

The women finished their entrees and ordered coffee and dessert – cappuccino crunch ice cream for two and Sandra's favorite, apple caramel nut pie, for the others – before turning back to the scenarios they had drafted. To refresh their memories, Sandra briefly summarized the report from the three women who had worked on the online dating scenario, and Laura did the same with Harriet's scenario about the murdered speaker. After considerable discussion, they finally moved toward a consensus.

"Though I think the online dating plot would be a lot of fun to work on, we're probably better equipped to write a story about the speaker in a retirement home. We know a lot more about that situation, and the dating scenario would take a lot of research," Barbara said.

"That's why it would be so much fun," Ellen said with a laugh. "But you're right – I think our chances of finishing a book about women in a retirement community are a lot better than they are with the other story outline. Do you all agree?"

Responses of "Sure," "Yes," and "Okay" came from around the table, so the decision was made. Sandra breathed a sigh of relief that the online dating idea could be put to rest and perhaps her unhappy dating experience with it.

"Okay, so what do we do? How do we get started?" Laura asked.

They all looked at each other for a minute before Sandra suggested, "I think we all need to write something down – perhaps a character or something about the setting. That way, we'll all be involved from the start."

This idea was eagerly accepted, and each one chose a character or some other element of the story to write up for the next Tuesday dinner. Sandra listed the tasks that each woman had volunteered for.

"I think we should take one piece from the other scenario," said Laura. "We should name the heroine Samantha. I don't know anyone with that name at Oakwood, and we can give her the nickname Sam."

"And her last name can be Spade," Sandra said laughing.

On that high note, the women headed to their apartments eager to start on their new adventure.

Sandra was the last to leave. She was glad there would be no more talk of online dating. She did not want to be reminded of that ever.

She wandered over to the auditorium where the movie was to be shown; she thought *Chariots of Fire* would be an enjoyable distraction. She had to sit at the back where there were a few empty seats. The man in the seat next to her offered her some popcorn. "I watched you come in," he said. The voice was vaguely familiar. She turned to look at him and was taken aback. *Coffee at the Chesapeake Grill!*

"It can't be you. Why are you here?" Sandra asked as the lights dimmed.

"Yes, it's me," he replied. "I've just moved in."

CHAPTER SIXTEEN

Surprise

*When one door of happiness closes, another opens,
but often we look so long at the closed door that we
do not see the one that has been opened for us.*
— HELEN KELLER

It was a cool, clear early spring morning when Robert set off for Washington. A morning like that was pleasant and relaxing especially since his troubles were behind him. He had a meeting to attend. It felt good that he was still needed occasionally and that the Alexei affair had not been held against him. After lunch, he planned to look for an appropriate wedding gift for Steve and Lindsey. Steve, who despite his diamond-in-the-rough demeanor, was knowledgeable about art. Not that he would presume to give Steve a painting, but he wanted to give him a gift in good taste and maybe useful too.

He thought about some of the weddings he had attended – often carefully planned and with no expense spared. Even as vows were being solemnly exchanged, he had wondered if the marriages would stand the tests of time, but he was looking forward to attending this wedding in a few weeks. It was one that would endure. He remembered the young and beautiful Laura in Italy who had impulsively married when she was still in college. *Much too young, but then, could one be too old? No fool like an old fool they say. Am I too old? Emphatically not. And no fool either!*

It was dark by the time he returned to Oakwood. He had spent a long time trying to find just the right gifts for the two people who had always been there for him. He carefully put his purchases away and sat down to a hearty dinner he had collected from the dining room. He watched the TV news and settled in his armchair to make his plans.

The next morning, he found Steve's address and called the jeweler to arrange for the delivery of the handsome clock he had purchased. He had left a card with the jeweler expressing his good wishes to be attached to the gift. He hoped it conveyed something of the genuine affection he felt for his constant and reliable friend. The second gift would await the right moment for him to give in person very soon.

Then he called Cathy. Cathy was not in the office when he called. Disappointed, he left a message that he would call again later. He would just have to wait.

The trouble with waiting is that it gives you time to think.

It was not until he learned that the mysterious dead man had been identified and the murderer found that he realized just how deeply he had been disturbed. Up to that point, all the challenges and intrigues he had had to deal with centered on other people's problems. He never imagined he would find himself seriously suspected of murder. For a while, the case against him looked menacingly convincing. While he had maintained his outward poise, he had been shaken by the idea that there were those who believed him to be capable of murder. He knew that his history might not have saved him if the authorities had believed he was guilty. Every phone call had brought with it the dreaded possibility of worse news. What a terrible way to end his career.

The relief he felt was overwhelming. His life was his own again without the need to be looking over his shoulder. He could get back to writing his book, something he could not have done while he was under suspicion even if he had had the file.

More than ever, he appreciated his good fortune to be living at Oakwood. He no longer thought so wistfully about the exhilarating life he had left behind. He had what he needed most – peace of mind and the company of people he had become fond of. It made him think of Harriet and Barbara, whose skills had been essential in solving the murder. Also, there was the remarkable fact that no word of the break-in and subsequent events had leaked out to the Oakwood community. The Tuesday Table Ladies had kept their word.

And then there was Cathy. Cathy, whom he had taken for granted, would always be there. And yet he had no idea what her plans were. Did she plan to retire? Where would she go? He had never asked her, and he wished he had. Their conversations, however pleasant, had never ventured that far. He had always thought of her as his friend's wife, but he could not imagine life at Oakwood without her.

He had for so long been on his own. But the other night when she had appeared dressed for dinner looking so elegant and independent, it had occurred to him that she might have plans that did not include Oakwood. Or him.

He called Cathy again. She was still away from her office. Dismayed, he left another message that he would call once again later.

Cathy was preoccupied with plans for renovating the Riverview dining room. She was meeting with the architect. She planned to take this opportunity to open the dining room to the lawn, which led down to the river. Residents would be able to take their lunch outside in good weather, and that would add another attractive feature to the campus. It would also provide a marketing advantage considering the increasing competition among retirement communities. The view was lovely.

She had invested a lot of herself in Oakwood. She had begun to think of it as her home. She felt deeply protective of it when Mrs. Cutler's apartment had supposedly been burgled. The break-in at Robert's cottage had been worse. She did not know whether she was more concerned for Oakwood or for Robert. He after all was so capable and calm and seemed to take it in stride. She had to admit, though, that he seemed withdrawn and deeply worried when matters took on the shape of murder. Not quite the debonair and resilient Robert she had known. But the threat to Oakwood was as real to Cathy as Robert's was to him.

It had all ended well for Oakwood and Robert. She was free to enjoy the prospect of a real improvement to the campus in the Riverview project and Robert's reprieve. She had not even dared to think of his being tried for murder. The break-in alone had been bad enough.

She had seen him very little since the evening when he had broken the bad news to her at dinner, but he had been much on her mind. So she was delighted when she found his phone messages on her return to the office. She wondered what was on his mind. *Three messages? He seems unusually persistent. No doubt he'll call again*, she thought.

It wasn't long before he did call again, and that time, Cathy was there to answer. What was on his mind was the hope that Cathy would accept an invitation for dinner, that time at an elegant restaurant a few miles beyond their favorite place.

"I wanted to celebrate the end of the troubles of the last few weeks. And I'm hoping you'll celebrate with me. Please don't say no. It must have been a worry for Oakwood too."

"The restaurant sounds rather fancy, Robert, but I've heard it's excellent. It's reputed to attract the more discriminating diners from Washington. Are you sure you don't want to go to our usual place?" It seemed to her such a change from their comfortable routine.

"No. I want a break from the past this time and do something more memorable. Besides, I think we've earned a great meal!"

"In that case, of course I'd love to go."

"I'll call for you on Saturday at five thirty."

"Bon soir, monsieur et madame." The maître d' called for their coats to be taken and led them to their table. Cathy paused to admire an exquisite bowl of spring flowers on a side table.

"Oui, madame, zey are beautiful, no? Finally, spring is arrived. It has been a winter most horrible. For us, business was slow. You come wiz spring, and we are most happy to welcome you."

He seated Cathy at the table and presented them with a menu in French consistent with the cuisine. "Your waiter, he is Paul."

Paul took their orders after letting them know the specialties of the house. "I beg of you, monsieur et madame, to be patient. We prepare everything fresh. We will serve a few appetizers for you while you wait." He summoned the sommelier. Robert carefully selected a Bordeaux red to accompany their meal. The sommelier approved his choice.

"Oh, Robert, this is really special. It feels like a long time since I was treated so royally."

"Well, I meant it to be special, Cathy. You see, it is you who are special." He paused waiting for her reaction. "And I now realize how much you've come to mean to me. During the past few weeks, I've been forced to take a good look at my life. In my mind, I've always seen you in terms of my wonderful old friend, your husband. Gary tragically left us years ago. We've moved on since then."

"We'll always love him, Robert, each in our own way. But you're right. I came to realize that I had to make a new life for myself months after he died. Otherwise, life would have had no meaning without him. I had no children who I suppose might have made a difference. So I developed a whole new life, which has been challenging and interesting. I know it's what he would have wanted for me, and I feel I have more good years ahead."

Robert nodded and waited while the hors d'oeuvres were served. "There are good years ahead of both of us. But here's how I feel about them. Cathy, I'd like to think you and I have so much to share now that life could be quite wonderful if we do."

Cathy smiled at him. He was so earnest. He scarcely seemed to have noticed just how much he meant to her. She waited for him to go on. But at that moment, the sommelier arrived with the wine. Robert sipped the taste the sommelier had poured for him and nodded appreciatively. Their glasses were filled.

"I should tell you that I too lost a great love years ago. I know I've never talked about her. She was an international journalist – young, handsome, and daring. She was like no one I had ever met before or since. She found her way to the front line of international events and was eventually killed in an ambush in the Far East. I was absolutely devastated and determined after that to live my life at a safer emotional level. And that's what I've done for far too long."

There was silence between them. Cathy was at a loss for words. She knew that Robert did not reveal his vulnerabilities, but that was what he had just done. It was a new level of intimacy to which she wanted to respond, but she didn't know what to say. She reached across the table and held his hand. He was so important to her, but she was uncertain where this was headed.

Robert's silence reflected the deep emotions of the moment. He knew that they were not temporary and that he needed to act on them. He touched the small box in his jacket pocket.

"Cathy, I don't know what your future plans are but I'm hoping you can feel the same way about me that I feel about you. I cannot now envision a life ahead without you. Is it possible that you could spend the rest of your life with me?"

Cathy held her breath and looked up at him with shining eyes.

Cathy smiled.

Epilogue

Here we say goodbye for now to the Tuesday Table Ladies of Oakwood and of course to Robert and Cathy too. They are a part of our lives, and we will miss them. They reflect how much we enjoy living in a retirement community. Perhaps they will inspire others to write their own stories or to make new friends, find new interests, write poetry, create art, sew quilts, or take up tai chi or bird-watching.

We have treasured the many letters and cards from readers who told us how welcome our books have been in the midst of depressing tales of old age. And we remember with joy the warm welcomes we received when invited to share the story of our writing adventures. But now, as Robert Frost wrote, we have promises to keep and miles to go before we sleep. We leave you with the following thoughts:

You can't use up creativity. The more you use,
the more you have.

—MAYA ANGELOU

In the end, it is not the years in your life that count.
It is the life in your years.

—ABRAHAM LINCOLN

About the Authors

Octavia Long is the pseudonym for six women who dine together every Tuesday at Longwood at Oakmont, a community of retirees in Western Pennsylvania. We continue to adhere to the following rules, which served us so well in writing our first book, *Where's Laura?*

1. All the authors have equal partnership in the project: none has any ownership of words, characters, or ideas.

2. This means there should be no hurt feelings when one's magnificent prose is edited or deleted.

3. This collaboration will stop only when it ceases being fun.

The following Tuesday Table Ladies joyfully collaborated in the planning and writing of this book:

Doreen E. Boyce
Anne K. Ducanis
Constance T. Fischer
Margaret L. Groninger
Jane L. Reimers
Muriel U. Weeks

WA